FROM THE
NANCY DREW FILES

THE CASE: A top-rated soap opera reaches a terrifying real-life climax when writer Karl Rudolph is murdered!

CONTACT: Nancy's old friend Sally Ling has been named assistant producer at *Love and Loss.*

SUSPECTS: Joe Ortega—*The associate writer always believed his ideas deserved more attention, and now he'll have his way.*

Aleta McCloud—*The glamorous star's character was about to be killed off and written out of the show . . . by Karl Rudolph.*

Yvonne De Young—*The show's director had been in a long and bitter feud with Rudolph . . . which may have come to a sudden, lethal end.*

COMPLICATIONS: Nancy finds herself in the spotlight on the set of *Love and Loss*—making her a perfect target for the murderer!

Books in The Nancy Drew Files® Series

#1	SECRETS CAN KILL	#68	CROSSCURRENTS
#2	DEADLY INTENT	#70	CUTTING EDGE
#3	MURDER ON ICE	#71	HOT TRACKS
#4	SMILE AND SAY MURDER	#72	SWISS SECRETS
#5	HIT AND RUN HOLIDAY	#73	RENDEZVOUS IN ROME
#6	WHITE WATER TERROR	#74	GREEK ODYSSEY
#7	DEADLY DOUBLES	#75	A TALENT FOR MURDER
#8	TWO POINTS TO MURDER	#76	THE PERFECT PLOT
#9	FALSE MOVES	#77	DANGER ON PARADE
#10	BURIED SECRETS	#78	UPDATE ON CRIME
#11	HEART OF DANGER	#79	NO LAUGHING MATTER
#16	NEVER SAY DIE	#80	POWER OF SUGGESTION
#17	STAY TUNED FOR DANGER	#81	MAKING WAVES
#19	SISTERS IN CRIME	#82	DANGEROUS RELATIONS
#31	TROUBLE IN TAHITI	#83	DIAMOND DECEIT
#35	BAD MEDICINE	#84	CHOOSING SIDES
#36	OVER THE EDGE	#85	SEA OF SUSPICION
#37	LAST DANCE	#86	LET'S TALK TERROR
#41	SOMETHING TO HIDE	#87	MOVING TARGET
#43	FALSE IMPRESSIONS	#88	FALSE PRETENSES
#45	OUT OF BOUNDS	#89	DESIGNS IN CRIME
#46	WIN, PLACE OR DIE	#90	STAGE FRIGHT
#49	PORTRAIT IN CRIME	#91	IF LOOKS COULD KILL
#50	DEEP SECRETS	#92	MY DEADLY VALENTINE
#51	A MODEL CRIME	#93	HOTLINE TO DANGER
#53	TRAIL OF LIES	#94	ILLUSIONS OF EVIL
#54	COLD AS ICE	#95	AN INSTINCT FOR TROUBLE
#55	DON'T LOOK TWICE	#96	THE RUNAWAY BRIDE
#56	MAKE NO MISTAKE	#97	SQUEEZE PLAY
#57	INTO THIN AIR	#98	ISLAND OF SECRETS
#58	HOT PURSUIT	#99	THE CHEATING HEART
#59	HIGH RISK	#100	DANCE TILL YOU DIE
#60	POISON PEN	#101	THE PICTURE OF GUILT
#61	SWEET REVENGE	#102	COUNTERFEIT CHRISTMAS
#62	EASY MARKS	#103	HEART OF ICE
#63	MIXED SIGNALS	#104	KISS AND TELL
#64	THE WRONG TRACK	#105	STOLEN AFFECTIONS
#65	FINAL NOTES	#106	FLYING TOO HIGH
#66	TALL, DARK AND DEADLY	#107	ANYTHING FOR LOVE

Available from ARCHWAY Paperbacks

The NANCY DREW

Files™
107

ANYTHING FOR LOVE

CAROLYN KEENE

AN ARCHWAY PAPERBACK
Published by POCKET BOOKS
New York   London   Toronto   Sydney   Tokyo   Singapore

This book is a work of fiction. Names, characters, places and incidents are products of the author's imagination or are used fictitiously. Any resemblance to actual events or locales or persons, living or dead, is entirely coincidental.

AN ARCHWAY PAPERBACK *Original*

An Archway Paperback published by
POCKET BOOKS, a division of Simon & Schuster Inc.
1230 Avenue of the Americas, New York, NY 10020

ISBN: 0-671-88198-1

First Archway Paperback printing May 1995

10 9 8 7 6 5 4 3 2 1

NANCY DREW, AN ARCHWAY PAPERBACK and colophon are registered trademarks of Simon & Schuster Inc.

THE NANCY DREW FILES is a trademark of Simon & Schuster Inc.

Cover art by Cliff Miller

Printed in the U.S.A.

IL 6+

ANYTHING FOR LOVE

Chapter

One

"Wow, THIS PLACE IS ADORABLE!" Bess Marvin exclaimed. "I never expected a bed-and-breakfast in New York City to be so—cozy. Good thing your aunt Eloise was out of town."

Nancy Drew's blue eyes sparkled. "You mean you aren't sorry we won't be staying in her elegant apartment?"

Bess shook her head. "No, I'm really glad Susan Ling's older sister was able to find this great garden apartment for us. And in the East Village, too. Susan said everything fun happens here."

"We are lucky," Nancy said. "I never dreamed that Sally Ling would offer to be our guide for our New York vacation."

"She's just like she was when we were in high school," Bess added. "Sally was always a big sister to all of us."

They happily surveyed the small but well-furnished living room. Two love seats were upholstered in a soft blue and white plaid, blending with the lush blue carpet.

"George is going to be so sorry she missed this trip," Bess added.

George Fayne, Bess's cousin, usually joined Nancy and Bess on vacations. But she couldn't leave River Heights because the girl's basketball team she was coaching had scheduled games.

Bess hurried into the next room. "Wait till you see the bedroom," she called back out. "Fluffy white down comforters on both twin beds."

Nancy carried her suitcase into the bedroom and grinned when she saw her friend stretched out on one of the beds. "We promised to call Sally to let her know we got in okay."

Bess popped up. "I'll do it," she said. "Maybe there's still time for her to show us around the studio today."

"I can't believe Sally is working on the number one soap opera, *Love and Loss,*" Nancy said, plopping down on her bed.

"Not just working on it. She's assistant to the executive producer." Bess picked up the phone on the nightstand and punched in the numbers. "We'll probably get the royal treatment."

"What kind of treatment is that?" Nancy

2

asked innocently, pretending she didn't know what Bess meant.

"You know. A limo and—" Bess stopped short and held up a finger as Sally came on the line. "Sally," Bess said, excitement raising her voice. "We're here—and we love this place."

Bess began to nod and reached for a pen, but then her expression changed. Nancy waited, wondering what Sally was saying. "What's wrong?" Nancy asked as soon as Bess hung up.

"There's been trouble on the show and security is extra tight," Bess said, frowning. "But Sally's going to try to get us clearance to visit."

"So what were you writing down?" Nancy asked.

"Directions to the uptown subway."

"What? No limo?" Nancy teased.

"Not this time," Bess admitted sheepishly. "But we are meeting Sally for a cappuccino at a little café near the studio. She promised to explain everything then."

Nancy patted her friend's blond head. "Don't worry. There's plenty to do in New York without getting on the set of a soap opera."

Bess smiled ruefully. "I was really hoping to get a good look at how a soap is put together."

"And maybe get a good look at how some of the actors are put together?" Nancy asked.

Bess grinned despite herself. "That could be a definite possibility."

Nancy unfastened the barrette holding her

ponytail. Her reddish blond hair swung free to her shoulders. "Anyway, it'll be fun taking the subway uptown like native New Yorkers."

Bess unzipped one of her suitcases. "What do you think we should wear, Nan?"

"For the subway?" Nancy teased. "Or for the soap opera hunks you still hope to meet?" She opened the suitcase on her bed. "I think I'll wear my purple sweater and long crinkly skirt. They're right on top."

"Great," Bess said. "I'll wear my royal blue tunic with the suede skirt. It fits perfectly—as long as I don't gain an ounce."

"Hope you have room for the cappuccino," Nancy said. Bess was always battling her sweet tooth.

After changing clothes and freshening their makeup, Nancy and Bess walked to the subway stop two blocks away. They squeezed into seats on the train, and soon they were climbing the stairs out of the subway stop near the studio. Chilled by the cool April breeze coming off the Hudson River, Nancy zipped up her leather jacket. Though she'd visited New York many times before, Nancy was still fascinated by the mixture of skyscrapers, old buildings, and little stores they passed.

"There's the café Coffee and . . ." Bess said. "An espresso will sure feel good right now."

The café sported a blue-and-green awning and large windows. Inside all the tables were taken.

Nancy looked around, but Sally hadn't arrived yet. She turned toward the entrance just in time to see a slender, dark-haired young woman hurry through the door.

"I hope you haven't been waiting long," Sally said, slightly out of breath.

"Just got here," Nancy said, smiling. "So relax, we may have a long wait for a table."

Bess blurted out, "Sally! You've changed your hair—you've got bangs. They look great."

Sally's brown eyes crinkled in pleasure. "Thanks. I was a little nervous about doing it—it takes so long to grow them out."

Nancy gave her friend a welcoming hug. "They're very becoming."

"You two are sure good for my ego," Sally said. "I wish we had more time to visit, but I have to get back soon." She pointed to the menu up on a chalkboard. "This place is known for its coffees and pastries. My favorite is the blueberry scone."

Bess groaned. "Don't tempt me."

"I'll stick with the cappuccino," Nancy said.

As the girls placed their orders at the counter, a table became available. "I'll grab it for us," Sally said. "You guys bring the coffee."

Once settled, Nancy thought she had detected anxiety in her friend's dark eyes, and decided to ask about her friend's problem. "Sally," Nancy said, leaning forward. "Bess mentioned that there's trouble at the studio. Could you tell us more about it?"

Sally hesitated, looking down. "Well," she said finally. "Our problem might not sound like much to you, but it's really very serious."

"Then it's serious to us, too," Nancy said.

Sally took a deep breath. "Okay. Someone's been leaking our show's story lines to *Soap Talk.*" Bess's blue eyes widened. "I read it. It tells everything you want to know about all the soap operas," she explained to Nancy.

"And some things we *don't* want you to know," Sally said, her tone grim. She then explained that the leaks in the magazine could hurt the show's high ratings. Viewers could stop watching if they knew how a major story was going to turn out. Then the networks would lose money because they charge advertisers according to the number of viewers a show has.

Nancy sipped her cappuccino thoughtfully. "So what you're saying is these leaks could eventually affect everyone's job on the show."

"Exactly," Sally said.

Bess brushed a wisp of blond hair behind her ear. "But I don't see why we can't visit the set, Sally. We don't know the story lines—so we couldn't possibly tell anyone."

"We've been barring all visitors," Sally said. "It's just a precaution—until we discover how the information is being passed on to a particular columnist." As Bess looked crestfallen, Sally smiled, obviously saving her news for a surprise.

"So I asked my boss, Peter Gardiner, to make an exception in your case."

"Did he?" Bess asked eagerly.

"Actually," Sally said, whipping out two passes from her purse, "he invited you to meet him in his office."

Bess beamed. "Isn't it lucky I wore my blue suede skirt!"

The girls returned their empty cups to the counter and then quickly made their way around the corner to the Premiere Broadcasting building. A good-looking young blond guy dashed out of the building and into a waiting cab. "Wow," Bess blurted out. "Is he a new actor on the show?"

Sally grinned, leading them into the building. "That's Zack, our music coordinator. He's a neat guy." In the lobby a security guard handed them a ledger to sign. They then continued on through heavy doors into a waiting elevator, where Sally punched a button for the third floor.

Peter Gardiner was a tall, rather gaunt man, with a few flecks of gray in his dark hair. His office, filled with paintings and sculpture, was twice the size of the entire apartment Nancy and Bess were staying in. He rose from behind an antique mahogany desk to greet his visitors. "You're the young detective Sally's been telling me about," he said, shaking Nancy's hand.

Nancy glanced at Sally, who avoided her eyes.

"This is my friend, and associate, Bess Marvin," Nancy responded. Whatever happened, she wanted to make sure that Gardiner included Bess.

Bess reddened slightly, appreciating Nancy's introduction. Nancy saw, with some amusement, that Bess kept glancing at the framed photos of actors on the wall. She stole a few glances herself as Gardiner repeated much of what Sally had already told them.

"These story line leaks are very rare in our industry," he said. "If an employee, at whatever level, is found to be the source, he or she would not only be fired, but would never again be hired by another show."

Nancy was pretty sure she knew what was coming. A glance at Bess showed that she, too, was expecting the same thing. Gardiner put their thoughts into words. "So, when Sally told me that you're an experienced detective, I hoped you'd be willing to look into this for us."

"Surely, there are other people you could ask," Nancy said. "I'm really in New York on vacation."

Gardiner frowned and ran his hand through his hair. "I understand your reluctance, Nancy. But if we bring in a total stranger, it would arouse suspicion, especially if the leak is coming from someone on the inside, as we're pretty sure it is. We can explain your presence more easily because you're a friend of Sally's."

Before he could say more, the door flew open, and a large, barrel-chested man, his face contorted with rage, charged into the office, waving a magazine above his shaved head. He slammed it down on Gardiner's desk and roared, "Either you stop that sneaky redheaded actress from destroying my work, or I'll destroy *her!*"

Then he whirled around and stalked out, leaving everyone in shocked silence.

Chapter

Two

"I'M SORRY I didn't have a chance to introduce you," Peter Gardiner said. His voice was calm, but his jaw was tight with anger. "That was Karl Rudolph, our head writer."

He picked up the magazine that had been thrown on his desk. "It's the latest issue of *Soap Talk*. I haven't had a chance to read it yet." He turned to Sally. "Have you?"

Sally reddened. "I'm afraid so. I didn't want to dump it on you as soon as you got in."

"Unlike Karl," Gardiner said. "Well, we might as well look at that so-called column, 'Our Best Guesses.'"

"I've read it," Bess said. "Whoever writes it has a pretty good track record in guessing."

"Unfortunately for us," Sally said, "these aren't 'guesses.'"

"I take it there's been another leak," Nancy said. Sally's expression confirmed it.

Gardiner had pulled a pair of glasses out of his breast pocket and began reading aloud: "'Gorgeous, redheaded Laura, a major character on the number one soap, *Love and Loss,* is going to be killed in an upcoming episode. A good guess says the killer is her estranged husband.'" The color drained from Gardiner's face.

Bess gasped. "Is that true?"

"I can't believe they would print such an important plot point," Gardiner said.

"You said there have been leaks before," Nancy pointed out.

Sally explained that the past leaks had been annoying, but not major. Nothing that would ruin a plot line.

"I guess that explains why Karl was in such a rage," Gardiner said.

"I understand how you all feel," Nancy said sympathetically. "It's no fun reading a mystery if somebody tells you how it ends."

Throwing the magazine into the wastebasket, Gardiner exploded, "The worst part is, we can't even change our story line. Not until we find out who's behind these leaks."

Nancy explained to a puzzled Bess. "Whoever is giving away the story line could do the same thing with a new ending."

"You can see our problem," Sally said to Nancy.

Nancy made another try at staying out of the investigation. "Just the fact that I'm Sally's friend wouldn't necessarily explain why I'm hanging around the studio," she said.

"Sally's come up with a cover story for you," Gardiner said as Nancy darted a quick, thanks-a-lot look at her dark-haired friend. Gardiner continued. "We could explain your presence by saying we've hired you as a consultant for an upcoming episode about a teen runaway. What do you think?"

"That's a wonderful idea," Bess said, then, catching Nancy's eye, added, "Sort of."

"Look," Nancy said. "I'm not sure I'm the right person for this job. But I'll hold off making a decision until I talk to some of your people."

Gardiner smiled. "Fair enough."

"And if I do decide to take the case, I'd also like to talk to the 'Our Best Guesses' columnist for *Soap Talk.*"

"I'm not sure that's a good idea," Gardiner said slowly. "First of all, he'd never reveal his source. And second, he might tip off the culprit and cause him or her to be more careful, making our job that much harder."

Nancy wasn't convinced it wouldn't help. "I could make up a reason for seeing him so he'd never know I was investigating the leaks," Nancy offered. "He'd certainly never reveal his source, but he might drop some clue without realizing it."

"Well, why don't you have a look around here first?" Gardiner suggested. "And even if you decide not to take the case, you'll learn a lot about soaps."

"I'll call and get ID cards made immediately," Sally said quickly. "Who do you want to talk to first?"

"I have to know who has access to the story lines, especially anyone who sees the stories in time to tip off a magazine columnist."

Sally and Gardiner said that *Soap Talk* would need the information about a month before publication.

"Story summaries, often called the bible, are prepared months, sometimes a year before they're written in script form," Gardiner explained. "The first people to see these summaries are myself and Sally. Next they go to the network people for final approval. Then the writing staff and casting director get copies.

"How about a typist?" Bess asked.

"Karl's a fanatic about secrecy," Sally said, rolling her eyes. "He does his own typing and makes his own copies. Then he gives them to us personally."

"Who else gets copies, besides the people you've mentioned?" Nancy asked, looking up from the pad on her lap.

"The set designers are next in line," Peter

Gardiner responded. "But the actors and directors don't know what's going to happen until they get their scripts."

"Which is . . ." Nancy prompted.

"About a week before we tape, or about two weeks before airtime."

"Not quite enough time to make a magazine's deadline," Nancy commented.

"Which rules them out, doesn't it?" Sally asked. "The actors and directors, I mean."

"Not really," Nancy said, putting her pen away. "I'd guess they could get hold of someone else's copy if they tried."

Sally and Gardiner admitted that would be possible. No one had ever been told to keep copies under lock and key—until now.

"So, Nancy," Mr. Gardiner said. "Who would you like to meet with first?"

"The two people most concerned with these leaks—Karl Rudolph, because the leaks ruin his story line, and the actress who plays Laura. She'll lose her job if her character gets killed off. I take it she's the redheaded woman Karl referred to?"

Sally nodded. "Aleta McCloud."

Nancy tapped her pad against her chin. "I imagine Aleta has the most to gain, then, if the story line is changed and her character lives."

"Absolutely," Gardiner said, impressed with Nancy's grasp of the situation.

"So that's why," Nancy continued, "Karl is accusing her of 'destroying his work.'"

Sally sighed. "It is a logical assumption. But actors lose their jobs all the time because of story lines. They accept it."

Nancy wondered just how easily actors really accepted it. "I'd like to start with Karl Rudolph," she decided. In response to Gardiner's raised eyebrow, she added, "I've found that when people are upset or angry, they often reveal more than they intend to. I might find out more if I talk to Karl now."

Sally led Nancy and Bess down to the main floor to Karl's office. "Will you forgive me for getting you into this?" she asked.

"Let's just say I owe you for being so nice to us younger kids in high school," Nancy said.

"I'll make it up to you," Sally said, stopping in front of a closed door. An ornate brass plate with the name Karl Rudolph on it faced them.

"Take a deep breath," Sally said, and knocked on the door. They heard Karl bark, "Come in." Sally shrugged apologetically. Once inside, she introduced Bess and Nancy as consultants for the teen-runaway story. Karl, his bald head shining, acted annoyed.

"I'm not working on that right now," he said. "I've got enough on my mind."

Nancy and Bess exchanged glances, while Sally tried to soothe the head writer. "Mr. Gardiner thought it would be a good idea for you to at least meet. He also hoped you could take Nancy and Bess on a brief tour of the studio."

Karl gave them a condescending nod. "Most of our women visitors prefer hair and makeup," he said.

Nancy controlled her irritation.

"I'll see you both later," Sally said, and took off with a quick wave to Nancy and Bess.

Karl leaned back in his swivel chair, crossing his long legs on a small stool in front of him. He wore chinos with a beige silk shirt, the sleeves rolled above his elbows. "Forgive the mess," he said, clearly not meaning it. "I'd ask you to sit down, but—" He waved a hand at his cluttered surroundings.

Nancy and Bess glanced around the crowded office. It wasn't that small, but every surface—the desk, a conference table, two small chairs, and even the floor—was covered with scripts. Floor-to-ceiling shelves sagged under books piled horizontally, using every inch of space.

"I like things handy," Karl said. "I can lay my hands on any script, tape, or book in thirty seconds. The beauty of my system," he went on, "is that nobody else can find anything."

"That must make you feel very secure," Nancy said, hoping to lead him into discussing the story leaks. It worked. Karl sat up abruptly, slamming his feet on the floor. As he did so, a photograph slid to the edge of the desk. Nancy saw that it was of a young blond woman.

"I *used* to feel very secure," he said. "Until some sneak undermined a year of my work."

"We saw that magazine article," Bess put in timidly.

"A piece of trash!" Karl exclaimed. Then he began pacing between the piles of scripts. "I'd fire that redheaded bimbo in a minute if I had proof she leaked my story line," he said.

"Aleta McCloud?" Nancy asked.

"She was never right for the role," he barked, running a hand over his bald head. "Ruined my whole concept."

"How could you fire her?" Nancy asked. "Wouldn't you need her for the final scenes?"

"We'd get a look-alike," Karl said angrily. "Ordinarily, I wouldn't want to do that for just a few months, but in this case it'd be worth it."

Bess mouthed the question "Look-alike?" to Nancy, but Nancy kept her attention fixed on Karl. "You're certain Aleta's the source of the leaks?"

"Who else?" Karl exploded. "Who else has motive. *Why* would someone murder? *Why* would someone steal? Answer the *why* and you've got your killer or your thief."

"Sometimes there are hidden motives," Nancy said.

Karl threw her an annoyed glance. "I *am* a writer," he said. "I don't need a lecture from you on motivation. Believe me, I know all the motives. But when the obvious one is staring you in the face, you don't have the luxury of casual curiosity. Besides, the most powerful motive of all is survival, and Aleta McCloud's survival on this show is at stake. She only got the job as a fluke."

"A fluke?" Nancy asked, sensing that this man's animosity went beyond the story leaks. But before Karl could respond, the phone rang. He answered briefly, then turned back to the girls.

"I'm wanted on the set. I bet it's a problem with the actress."

He started to leave, then remembered. "Oh, yeah. The tour. Look, I'll walk you up to hair and makeup and then get someone to take over."

"Don't worry about us," Nancy said, her tone lightly tinged with sarcasm.

Karl didn't pick up on it. "No problem. Let's go."

With Nancy and Bess hurrying to keep up, Karl strode down another long corridor and up a flight of stairs. Stopping in front of a partially open door, he motioned the girls in first. So the man does have some manners, Nancy thought.

Bess entered, just as a figure seated in a barber's chair slowly turned toward the door. The woman's long red hair hid her face, and her head hung down at an odd angle. Nancy, right behind Bess, could see only the back of the person's head in the mirror. As the head slowly tilted, Bess suddenly screamed!

Chapter

Three

N<small>ANCY, SHE'S DEAD!</small>" Bess shrieked, and turned away, covering her mouth with her hand.

The bright lights in the room blinded Nancy for a moment. Then her gaze focused on the figure in the barber's chair. The long red hair hid most of the face, but blood was apparently flowing from the mouth or throat. Nancy noticed that the large cape used to protect clothing during makeup application concealed the person's body. Only a bloodstained hand and black cowboy boots were visible.

Before Nancy could move into the room, Karl pushed past them. "Relax, girls. It's not what you think," he said matter-of-factly. He strode directly over to the figure and grabbed a handful of the red hair. With a forceful yank he pulled on the hair, which turned out to be a wig. "Let me introduce the cast clown, Steve Basset. This is just another one of his stupid pranks."

"Sorry I frightened you," Steve said, laughing. He tossed aside the makeup cape. "Just killing time before I'm needed on the set. I had planned to surprise the makeup staff." Taking a cloth, he wiped the artificial blood off his neck. "They're on break and should return any time now."

Karl introduced Nancy and Bess to Steve. "When he's not being a jerk, he plays—"

"Troy Parker," Bess blurted out, gazing at the handsome actor, "my favorite character on the show."

"Thanks," Steve replied with a charming smile, stepping away from the chair to shake their hands.

Karl tossed the wig at Steve. "Put this back where it belongs," he barked.

Steve gazed pointedly at Karl's shaved head. "Sure you don't want to keep it?"

"Basset, take over the girls' tour. I'm wanted on the set." Then, with a sarcastic edge to his voice, he added, "And Basset, since you'd rather kill time than memorize your lines, your performance had better be word perfect."

"Whew!" Bess said after Karl had left the room. "Is he always so intense?"

"Karl's never much fun to be around," Steve said, wiping a spot of fake blood off his boots.

"Right now there's a lot going on to give ol' Rudy grief."

"I understand a story leak can ruin a show's rating," Nancy said, taking the opportunity to probe.

Steve casually ran his hand through his thick dark hair. "Then you've heard about the leaks. Hard to believe. There's not much anyone connected with the show has to gain. That person would be as good as dead in this business." Steve slid a finger across his throat for emphasis. Bess laughed.

Nancy was intrigued by this young actor's attitude. Was he really just a "clown"?

"So," Steve went on more briskly, "what's this VIP tour about?"

"Mr. Gardiner asked Nancy to act as a consultant for the runaway-teen story you'll be doing," Bess said, pride in her voice. Steve's eyes widened as he looked at Nancy. "I take it you've been a runaway teen?"

"Not really," Nancy said, laughing.

"But Nancy's a detective, and she knows about those things," Bess volunteered, then glanced at Nancy, wondering if she'd said too much.

"Nancy's also on vacation," Nancy said, "and Mr. Gardiner promised us a tour."

Steve bowed, then motioned them to the barber-style chairs. "Bess, Nancy, take a seat. Your studio tour is about to start." The girls exchanged smiles as they sat down. "The magic of show business begins in these chairs," Steve went on as he gently slipped the red wig on Bess's head. "One, two, three—like magic, you're transformed into a fiery redhead."

Bess looked in the mirror, pleased with the change. "I like it," she said, twirling a lock of the hair around a finger.

"So do I," Steve said with a charming smile.

Nancy caught the meaning in his tone and saw her friend's face redden as Steve's dark eyes lingered on Bess.

Just then a woman's voice came from behind them, interrupting the moment. "Well, I don't like it! Take off my wig. Now!"

They all turned in the direction of the voice. Standing at the threshold was Aleta McCloud, wearing dark glasses, her long red hair pulled back in a ponytail. "If you're here to audition for my role, forget it. I'm not off this show yet."

Bess turned as red as the wig she hastily pulled off her head. Nancy and Bess stepped down from the chairs, making sure they were out of the actress's path.

"Now, Aleta," Steve said, not taking her seriously, "let's not get hysterical and blow this out of proportion." He quickly introduced the girls to Aleta as story consultants. "I'm showing them some behind-the-scenes magic," he added.

"I haven't got time for nonsense like this. I'm scheduled to be on the set in ten minutes for camera blocking," Aleta muttered in frustration. "Where's Bobbie? She's supposed to make me up."

"Bobbie's our makeup magician," Steve began, just as a short, chubby woman in a light blue smock bustled into the room, her high heels tapping on the tile floor. "And here's the genius in person."

"Take it easy, sugar," Bobbie said matter-of-factly to Aleta. "I'm ready when you are." She threw a dry glance at Steve. "You're wanted on the set pronto, mister. I hope you weren't messin' with my potions."

"Never," Steve said solemnly. "Guess that finishes my end of the tour," he added to the girls. "But don't despair. I'm sure Aleta can do almost as well, in the ten minutes she has left."

He saluted them and left. As soon as he was gone, Aleta turned to Bess, who was still holding the wig. "I don't do tours. And would you please put my wig back on its stand?"

Obliging Aleta, Bess placed the wig on an empty stand. Nancy shrugged and shook her head, deciding they'd better not try to explain the wig story.

"What's got you so fired up?" Bobbie asked, quickly dabbing makeup on Aleta's face.

"There was another major story leak in that magazine column today. As usual, Rudolph is trying to pin it on me," Aleta responded caustically. "And the stress is making my hair fall out."

"I noticed," Bobbie said. "There's been an awful lot of extra hair in your brush lately."

Just then Sally appeared in the doorway, gesturing for Nancy and Bess to come into the hall. "I see you've already met Aleta," Sally commented, once Nancy and Bess had joined her outside the makeup room.

"You might say we've had that pleasure," Nancy said dryly.

"In any case," Sally went on, "I wanted to give you an update on some plans. First, since tomorrow's Saturday, Steve and I thought we'd all get together—"

"Does that 'all' include Nancy and me?" Bess asked excitedly.

"Of course," Sally replied with a grin. "Unless you'd rather not."

"Are you kidding? Can't you hear my heart pounding?" Bess asked with a laugh. "Steve Basset's a hunk. What girl wouldn't want to hang out with him?"

"What do you have planned?" Nancy asked, curious.

"We're meeting in Central Park," Sally said. "We can rent in-line skates there to go blade skating. It's a great way to take in the park and get exercise, too."

Bess's hand flew to her face. "I don't have a thing to wear."

Nancy smiled. "I have a hunch Bess would like to interrupt our tour for a bit of shopping."

Bess giggled. "You don't mind, do you? I saw a Bloomingdale's ad on the plane. It showed the cutest skating outfits."

"By all means, take a shopping break. The tour can wait," Sally said, waving her hand. "There's nobody free right now anyway. But come back when you're finished to meet the other people on the show.

"Oh, and one more thing," she continued cheerfully. "Would you like to have dinner tonight at a great new restaurant? A friend of mine is coming—a girl," she added quickly.

"Don't look at me," Bess replied with a grin. "I'll admit that girls can be fun, too." She gave Nancy a playful punch, and the two girls waved goodbye to Sally and headed for the elevators.

A couple of hours later Nancy and Bess stepped out of Bloomingdale's and walked briskly down Lexington Avenue toward Fifty-seventh Street. The spring breeze tugged at Bess's big brown shopping bag, which held her new skating outfit, as well as a new purple cardigan sweater. At the corner the girls headed crosstown to catch a bus back to the West Side. When they got off, they headed up Columbus Avenue, enjoying a bit of window-shopping. The street was lined with trendy shops of all kinds.

"Isn't that dress adorable?" Bess said, admiring a flowered print dress with a lace collar on display in the window of one of the boutiques. Nancy agreed but preferred the simple lines of a pair of turquoise leggings with matching angora sweater in the next window. Then, changing the subject, Bess asked, "Don't you think Steve Basset has the warmest brown eyes you've ever seen?"

"Um-hmm." Nancy nodded, adding, "Only if you don't include a cocker spaniel puppy." Nancy could tell that Bess was getting a crush on the actor. She also knew what was coming next.

"I think he likes me," Bess said hopefully. "I know we just met, but . . ."

As they continued window-shopping, Nancy tried to put her thoughts in order. She decided she had to discover the motive for the leaks before she could uncover their source. She also wondered how long she could keep up her ruse as a consultant to the studio.

Suddenly Bess stiffened. "Nancy, stop!" Bess cried out. "Don't take another step."

Nancy stopped and turned to see Bess pointing at something in the window of a little shop. "What's the matter, Bess?" Nancy asked. Then she saw what was making Bess so excited: a black velvet baseball cap with a long red ponytail attached to the back.

"I've got to have it! Come on." Bess grabbed Nancy's arm as she pushed open the glass door and stepped into the shop.

"The cap in the window—I'd like to try it on, please," Bess told the woman behind the counter.

"I have one here." The woman pulled it off the rack and handed it to Bess. "You'll love it."

Bess pushed her hair up underneath, then pulled the cap down low on her forehead. "It's perfect." Bess beamed with delight, checking herself in the mirror. "I've always wanted red hair, and this looks so real. Just like I'm wearing my own hair in a ponytail."

"I take it you plan to wear it back to the studio," Nancy remarked with a grin, smoothing the fake hair.

"Sure, maybe I'll run into Steve. I'd love to get his reaction." Bess smiled at the thought of the handsome actor.

Nancy and Bess returned to the sidewalk and did a little more window-shopping. "I think we'd better hurry," Nancy finally said. "The sooner we get to know who's who at the studio, the sooner we can figure out what's behind this mystery."

Bess nodded. "I don't see how Karl Rudolph can avoid changing his story line if—"

Suddenly Nancy put her hand on Bess's arm. "Don't look back," she warned. "There's a man following us!"

Chapter

Four

WALK TO THE NEXT BOUTIQUE and then stop," Nancy said in a low voice. "Pretend to be window-shopping."

"How do you know he's following us, Nan?" Bess's voice shook a little.

"I first spotted him after we came out of the store where you bought your new hat. He's stopped each time with us," Nancy said. As casually as possible, the girls peeked in at the next shop. Nancy discovered that a mirror used in the window display gave her a strategic view of the short, stocky man with the black mustache. He was glancing at them furtively. Nancy pretended to fix her hair in the mirror, while watching him.

"He's still with us, Bess," she whispered.

"We've got to keep moving to find out what he's up to."

As they continued walking, Nancy could hear his footsteps moving closer. When she guessed he was right behind them, she whirled around to face him. Startled, the man stopped just as abruptly. Nancy's eyes locked on his. When Bess turned, he stared at her for a moment, then spun and hurried off the way he had come.

The girls followed as fast as they could, dodging passersby and stepping around window-shoppers. But when they reached the first corner, there was no sign of the short stranger.

Bess groaned. "Where could he have gone?"

Nancy bit her lip in frustration. "He might have ducked into another shop, or even into a taxi."

"Why would a stranger follow us?" Bess asked, straightening her new cap, which had slipped during their run.

"I think he may have mistaken one of us for someone else," Nancy surmised. "Actually, he didn't dash off until you turned around."

"Maybe from the back, the ponytail and cap make me look like someone he knows," Bess suggested.

"That's possible." Nancy raised her arm to flag a taxi. "Just in case he's loitering nearby, we'd better take a cab the rest of the way."

After a brief cab ride, Nancy and Bess pushed through the glass revolving doors of Premiere

Broadcasting. At the security guard's desk, they showed their passes and signed the ledger. Then they stepped into an elevator and pushed the button for the third floor.

Sally's office was two doors down from Peter Gardiner's. She looked up from her desk and squealed when she saw Bess. "You didn't get that cap in Bloomie's!" she said with a wide grin.

"Nope," Bess said, swinging her head so the ponytail moved back and forth. "On Columbus Avenue. Cute, huh?"

"It's you," Sally said firmly.

Nancy was standing a bit behind Bess as the two girls talked about the new cap. The fake ponytail looked real. Testing her theory, she asked Bess to turn her back toward Sally. "Sal, who does Bess remind you of?" Nancy asked her friend.

"With that red ponytail . . . it could be Aleta, I guess. Or any redheaded woman. Why?" Sally replied.

"Just a thought," Nancy said. "Red hair is so eye-catching. It's often the first thing you notice about a person."

"I'd like to see if someone else notices," Bess said, tossing her head.

"Now, who could you possibly mean?" Nancy asked, her blue eyes sparkling with fun.

"Darned if I know," Sally said, playing along. "But I think Steve's scene is about to be taped. How would you two like a quick visit?"

Bess was the first one out the door as Sally led them back down to the main floor, through a very long corridor toward the taping studio. "We call the whole building 'the studio,'" Sally said. "But the area they shoot the scenes in is the real studio. We can't go in if they've started taping."

Bess groaned. "How will we know?"

They were approaching the closed door of the studio as Sally pointed. "See that red bulb over the door? If it's lit, it means they're taping and we can't go in. If it's not—"

"It's *not!*" Bess said excitedly.

"Then we can go in," Nancy said, then added teasingly, "That is, if you want to, Bess."

Bess made a little face at her friend as Sally pushed open the door and gestured for them to follow her into the huge cement-walled room.

The activity inside was incredible. Techies were positioning huge cameras, while stagehands locked scenery together. Cast and crew clustered together in small groups, exchanging last-minute directions. In one corner of the room was the set of Troy Parker's bedroom, where the next scene was about to be shot. A set dresser was fussing with the pillows to make the bed look slept in.

"It looks so different on TV," Bess said. "The room seems much smaller here."

Off to one side stood Steve Basset. Bobbie was touching up his makeup as he glanced over the pages of script he held. He looked up for a moment and did a double-take when he caught

31

sight of Bess. He walked over to Nancy and Bess immediately.

"I almost didn't recognize you," Steve said with a grin, eyeing Bess's cap. "You're a knockout with red hair. Of course, I thought that even when you had blond hair."

"Show-biz magic," Bess said, laughing.

"Places, please," a voice announced over the speaker system. "One minute to tape."

"I have to take off," Sally said. "You can watch for a while. Afterward, why don't you go to the casting director's office? It's on this floor. Near Karl's office."

She left, and Nancy turned back in time to see Steve run off with Bess's cap in his hand. "What's Steve up to?" she asked.

Bess shrugged, beaming at him.

"Quiet on the set," came the order over the speaker system. This was the cue for the assistant director to begin the countdown. In the silence of the studio Nancy felt the tension take hold.

"Cameras rolling!" the assistant director yelled. "Scene five, take one. And in four . . . three . . . two . . ," Nancy held her breath. In a split second Steve Basset the clown would become the cool Troy Parker. But before the assistant director could say "one," laughter broke out on the set. Nancy and Bess giggled as they exchanged glances. The assistant director yelled, "Cut! Basset, take off that ridiculous cap!"

Bess grinned. "I see what he meant."

Nancy watched the actors on the set. Some were smiling, but the assistant director clearly was not amused. His voice boomed over the mike. "Let's do it again, people. Without Mr. B's improvisations. And clear the set, please!"

"I think that's our cue to leave, Bess," Nancy whispered, shouldering her purse. She and Bess tiptoed out of the studio. "Sally said the casting director's on this floor, near Rudolph's office." Nancy pointed toward one end of the corridor. "I think it's that way."

As they headed down the hall, they began hearing loud voices. As they got closer, Nancy recognized Karl Rudolph's voice. They stopped outside his office door. "Rewrite it!" Rudolph was shouting. "You write what I tell you."

"You don't get it, do you?" another man's voice shouted back from behind the closed door. "You're making a big mistake."

"Then it's *my* mistake. Get that?"

The office door burst open just then, and an attractive dark-haired man in a blue chambray workshirt stalked past them.

Nancy peered inside the office. It was even more disheveled than before. Karl Rudolph caught her eye. "What do you want?" he barked, obviously upset.

"Just looking for—" Nancy began, but Rudolph wasn't in the mood to listen.

"I've got my hands full at the moment," he responded gruffly. "Track down Joe Ortega. Tell him I said he's to assist you." Focusing his attention on the stack of papers in front of him, he muttered, "Now close the door. I've got a deadline."

Nancy closed the door and then turned back to Bess. "Let's see who we can find first," Bess offered. "The casting director or Joe Ortega, whoever he is."

They continued down the corridor. Near the elevator they noticed a strip of cardboard in a brass holder. It read, Joseph Ortega. Nancy knocked, and a voice called out, "Barge in. Everyone else does!"

Nancy opened the door. Working at a computer was the man who had just left Karl Rudolph's office.

Joe looked up frowning, then gave a small embarrassed smile, clearly recognizing them. "Sorry you had to witness that outburst. The guy can really push my buttons."

Nancy introduced herself and Bess as consultants hired by Peter Gardiner to work on a teenage-runaway story.

"Karl Rudolph suggested that you might help us," Nancy told him, noting the neatly stacked scripts on his desk. Apparently, this writer didn't share Karl's appetite for clutter.

"Actually, we've done quite a bit of research already," Joe said, somewhat apologetically. "We just can't decide if our main runaway should be a male or female. Do you have any thoughts on that?"

Nancy caught Bess's apprehensive glance. They hadn't really discussed story possibilities. Nancy pulled out her notebook. "On a recent case," she said, pretending to read from her pad, "a brother *and* sister in their early teens ran away from home."

Joe smiled. "Now, there's one idea we hadn't considered." Then his expression darkened, and he added, "Which means it probably won't fly."

"Why not?" Bess asked.

Joe shook his head. "Rudolph isn't receptive to anyone else's opinion. I suggest you don't knock yourselves out working on this. It's a waste of time. Rudolph's on the warpath."

"Isn't he just upset about the leaks?" Bess ventured.

"Paranoid is more like it," Joe said, his dark eyes narrowing. "Rudolph has turned this problem into a vendetta. He isn't satisfied with just killing off the character of Laura. He's also trying to ruin Aleta McCloud's career by pinning the blame on her. And heaven help anyone who stands in his way." Joe suddenly gestured to the small sofa across from his desk. "Forgive my manners. Please, sit down."

Nancy and Bess sank gratefully onto the cushions. "It seems to me there's little that can be done to save Laura's character," Nancy probed.

"As long as Rudolph's in the picture," Joe responded. "Just so you know, I've written a better story line. One that doesn't involve killing Laura."

"Have you told anyone about it?" Nancy asked.

"Peter Gardiner and Karl—maybe a few others. But Karl won't even consider it," Joe said, making a fist and punching the top of his desk.

"Too bad," Bess put in. "I think Aleta McCloud is perfect in the role of Laura."

Joe brightened. "She is talented. It would be a loss to the show if she were written out."

Nancy glanced at her watch. "You've been very helpful. But it's getting late, and we want to meet with the casting director."

"Rochelle Foster," Joe said. "Her office is across the hall, past the elevator."

Nancy and Bess stood up, thanked him, then headed for Rochelle Foster's office. When they got there, the door was open. Peeking inside, the girls saw a striking woman in her early forties. She sat on her desk talking on the phone, a large topaz ring sparkling on her finger.

Nancy had a hunch the woman was once an actress. There was something flamboyant in her manner. Without interrupting the flow of her conversation, Rochelle smiled warmly and gestured to the girls to come in and take a seat. A large cork board covering one wall caught their attention. Dozens of glossy headshots were pinned to it. Nancy imagined that each picture was of an actor or actress who hoped to be cast on the soap. "Stop me if I'm wrong, but you must be Nancy Drew and Bess Marvin?" Rochelle asked, smiling warmly as she hung up. "I'm Rochelle, sorta the mom around here. What can I do for you?"

"Sally Ling was giving us a tour, but she had to return to her office," Nancy said.

"That was Sally on the phone. She says you're consulting on the runaway story." As she spoke, Rochelle began rummaging through a stack of photos on the nearby credenza. "I've got some headshots here of possible runaways—"

Just then Nancy realized Rochelle's elbow was about to knock over a silver framed photo. Moving quickly, Nancy grabbed the frame before it fell.

"Clumsy me," Rochelle said good-naturedly. "My mother always said I had more beauty than grace."

Before putting the frame back on the credenza, Nancy noticed the photo was of a girl about eight years old, standing next to a horse-drawn carriage on a busy New York street.

"That's my little girl," Rochelle commented, looking at the photo with a mother's pride. "Well, I guess she's not so little anymore." Returning her attention to Nancy and Bess, she added, "Maybe we'd better forget the runaway pictures for now. If they kill Laura off, they might kill the runaway story line, too."

"So you really think Karl plans to kill me?" a voice asked from the doorway. They all turned to see Aleta standing there.

"I don't have a crystal ball, Aleta," Rochelle said. "But come on in and meet—"

"We've met," Aleta interrupted flatly. "What I meant was—do you think Karl will change his story line because of the leaks?"

"Same answer," Rochelle said. "Don't know."

Aleta turned to Bess and Nancy, as if seeing them for the first time, Nancy felt. "You're the only people I haven't asked," Aleta said. "I'm sure you've heard about the notorious leaks." Nancy and Bess nodded uneasily. Aleta went on. "Rochelle is too nice to say so, but I'm Karl Rudolph's prime suspect. The question is—will it affect what Rudolph does? Since you're a story consultant, Ms. Drew, what's your best guess?"

"I suppose," Nancy began slowly, "that it depends on what's best for the show."

"You're not a consultant," Aleta said coldly. Nancy stiffened as Aleta added, "You're a lame diplomat."

"That's enough, Aleta," Rochelle chided gently. "I have to run out for a minute. Dare I leave you alone with these two nice young ladies?"

Aleta shrugged and Rochelle excused herself. When she was gone, Nancy turned to Aleta. "You make it sound as though Karl Rudolph has it in for you. Have you done anything to make him angry?"

"Nothing," Aleta replied, but Nancy noticed a flicker of uneasiness in her eyes. "He never wanted me for the role of Laura. It was Yvonne De Young, one of the directors, who brought me to Peter Gardiner's attention. I auditioned for him and was hired. Rudolph was really steamed at not being able to make the choice so he never accepted me and he never forgave Yvonne. But Rudolph found a way to get even with her," she continued spitefully. "Karl Rudolph always pays people back."

"Could the leaks be someone's way of getting even with Karl?" Nancy asked mildly.

Aleta acted intrigued. "Maybe." Then her expression darkened, her eyes gleaming. "One thing I know for sure. It's time someone taught Karl Rudolph a lesson—he can't keep playing God with people's lives!"

Chapter

Five

D<small>ON'T PEOPLE EVER TRY</small> to get even with Karl?" Nancy asked.

"I've never heard of anyone succeeding," Aleta said. Then she smiled slyly as she added, "Of course, there's a first time for everything."

"I didn't realize a writer could be that powerful," Bess said.

"He's not just a writer," Aleta said. "He's a *head* writer. He creates the stories. On our soap that makes you king. Especially since the ratings are high."

"And *Love and Loss* is number one," Nancy said.

"So far," Aleta said pointedly. Then she shrugged and left. Graciousness was not the actress's strong suit, Nancy noted.

"What do you think, Nan?" Bess asked.

Nancy walked over to Rochelle's desk. "You mean, do I think that Aleta's the leak?" Nancy said. After Bess nodded, Nancy went on thoughtfully. "I think that being an actress means constant insecurity. And to quote a certain writer: 'Motive' is the key."

"Aleta's motive being to save her job," Bess declared.

"Or to get even. The problem is," Nancy added, pushing a reddish blond curl away from her face, "it's such an obvious motive."

"Then you don't think she's the one?"

"I'd like to be sure," Nancy said. "But right now I'll settle for going back to our cozy B and B and changing for dinner. I'll just give Sally a ring to check the plan."

Bess brightened as she stood up. "That's right. Sally said we're going to a neat new restaurant."

Nancy picked up the phone and confirmed dinner with Sally. Then Nancy and Bess gathered their purses and left the studio, heading for the subway.

Once back in their apartment Nancy tossed her purse on the bed and sat down next to it. "I'm so glad we're not meeting Sally for dinner until eight."

Bess plopped down on the other bed. "Especially since we didn't leave the studio until after six. I can't believe the hours those people keep. Even on a Friday."

"They shoot an episode a day," Nancy said, kicking off her shoes and propping up some pillows behind her. "No matter how long it takes."

"So what're we going to wear?" Bess asked.

"I bet you're going to wear your new sweater," Nancy said with a knowing smile.

"Isn't it the most heavenly shade of purple?" Bess reached for the Bloomingdale's shopping bag.

"You can borrow it whenever you like," Bess offered, then added quickly, "unless, of course, I'm wearing it."

"Oh, Bess, how can you be so unfair?" Nancy asked teasingly. She gave her friend a warm smile. "I think I'll wear my black miniskirt with the green silk blouse that Ned gave me."

After resting and showering, the two friends felt revitalized and ready for their evening out. Sally came for them, bubbling with enthusiasm for the restaurant she'd chosen. Not only did it specialize in unusual salads, she said, but the owner, a popular woman chef, was a fan of "Love and Loss."

"She's even named her salads after the characters on the soap," Sally declared. "So don't be surprised if you see some of the people who work on our show eating there. We feel it's our special place."

"You make New York sound like a small town," Bess said, her eyes sparkling with anticipation.

"In some ways it is," Sally said, smiling. "Manhattan *is* an island, after all. And people who work together often hang out together. I think you'll really like my friend Ellen Powell," she added. "She's an actress, but she's not totally self-absorbed like some actresses. Ellen's really interested in other people and what they do."

The restaurant was located in an old brownstone, making it homey yet elegant. Tall bay windows were framed in moss-green velvet draperies that contrasted with delicate ivory lace café curtains. The chairs were upholstered in green velvet while the linen tablecloths were ivory and green, with a pattern that resembled English ivy climbing on a trellis.

"This is so charming," Nancy said as the waiter seated them.

"You match the decor perfectly, Nan," Bess said.

"I love that soft green on you, too," Sally said. "It really goes with your hair—"

"Ahem," Bess said, preening a bit.

Sally laughed. "Your purple cardigan sets off your hair, too, Bess. I can't wait for my friend Ellen to meet my stylish friends from River Heights."

As if on cue, a voice behind them said, "And that's no exaggeration. They're real knockouts."

"Ellen!" Sally exclaimed.

Bess and Nancy turned to see a slender, brown-haired girl wrapped in a rose chenille shawl that matched her knit sheath perfectly and set off her green eyes. Ellen smiled warmly at them as she touched Bess's shoulder. "I have that same sweater," she said, "but I think it looks better on a blond."

Bess blushed, obviously pleased. Sally happily introduced them, adding a few remarks about everyone's background. Nancy and Bess learned that Ellen was an actress who'd grown up in California. She was familiar with New York from visiting her grandparents who lived in Brooklyn Heights. She'd moved recently, hoping to land a job.

"The competition is really fierce in Hollywood," Ellen said. "Not that it isn't a struggle in New York. But there's a feeling of community here—as if we're all in it together."

"That's good to hear," Bess said. "Especially after the earful we got today about people doing anything to survive." She glanced worriedly at Sally. "I hope I'm not speaking out of turn."

"Not at all," Sally said with a smile. "Karl's reputation extends well beyond our studio. But I think we'd better order now."

"Everything's delicious," Ellen said. "Even if none of the dishes are named after me."

"*Yet,*" Sally added loyally.

"Actually," Ellen said, opening her menu, "I

was a day-player once on *Love and Loss,* but I guess that doesn't count."

"Day-player?" Bess asked.

Ellen smiled. "Sorry. We get so used to our own jargon, we forget that everyone doesn't speak soap talk. A day-player," she explained, "works for a day at a time on a show, usually filling a small role. I was lucky," she added, "I had lines to speak that time. In fact, even though the part was small, I use the tape of my performance to show other casting directors."

"That was before I began working on the show," Sally said. "I didn't know Ellen then."

"How did you two meet?" Nancy asked.

"Through Steve. He and Ellen are friends." For Ellen's benefit, Sally launched into the story of Steve's latest practical joke. Bess looked a bit uneasy, and Nancy felt sorry, knowing her friend was probably wondering if Ellen and Steve were more than just "friends."

"I think I'll have the Briny Brigit salad," Nancy said, hoping to distract Bess. "How about the rest of you?"

The Briny Brigit combined unusual field greens and tiny shrimp. Bess and Sally settled on the Molly Medley, a mixture of fresh vegetables and char-broiled strips of chicken. Ellen finally picked the Laura Light, with asparagus and tuna in a clear lemon dressing.

"Leave room for dessert," Sally reminded them.

Nancy grinned at Bess's wistful expression. "We can split one," Nancy offered reassuringly.

Bess brightened. "Right."

"So, you've already met the prickly Karl Rudolph," Ellen said. "I had that pleasure when I was a day-player for the show." Ellen went on to admit that she'd seen the recent issue of *Soap Talk* and was shocked to read the latest revelation.

As the others continued talking, Nancy glanced idly around the large dining room until a blaze of red hair caught her eye. Way in the back Aleta and Joe had just stood up, apparently ready to leave. As Nancy turned back to tell the others, she noticed a man standing near the restaurant entrance. She recognized him as the man who'd been following her and Bess earlier. He was now staring toward the back of the room. Following his gaze, Nancy realized he was watching Aleta and Joe. When she glanced back, the man was leaving the restaurant with a tall woman who was wearing a wide-brimmed red hat that hid her face.

"You won't believe this," Nancy said. But before she could explain, Joe had approached their table.

"Well, well, well," he said. "Look who's here."

"I told you," Sally said to Nancy and Bess. "This is L and L's hangout."

"You weren't gossiping, were you, Sally?" Joe

asked in a teasing tone. Before Sally could respond, Joe stared more closely at Ellen. "Have we met?" he asked. "You look awfully familiar."

Ellen shook her head. "Sorry."

Sally suggested that Joe might have seen Ellen when she was a day-player on the show. Joe shrugged. "That's probably it," he said.

By this time Aleta had emerged from the ladies' room and joined Joe. "I'm ready to leave," she murmured to him, then nodded at the others.

After Aleta and Joe had left, Nancy wondered if Aleta was always so unfriendly.

"She probably was nicer before a salad was named after her," Sally said.

They laughed, but Bess, trying to be charitable, said that Aleta was probably just tense. Then she stopped and looked at Sally, hoping she hadn't said too much.

"How come?" Ellen asked. Then, as Sally hesitated, Ellen put it together. "Oh, no. Do they suspect Aleta of leaking the information?" Sally slowly nodded.

"Oh, my," Ellen said. "You mentioned that Nancy was a detective in River Heights. Is she investigating?"

Sally tried to cover her slip. "Nancy's consulting with the writers about one of our new story lines. But we'd just as soon no one from the show hears about her other work—"

"Don't worry, Sal," Ellen interrupted, putting her hand Sally's shoulder. "I won't say anything. It's none of my business, anyway."

"Actually," Bess jumped in, "I understand you know Steve Basset."

Ellen laughed. "Stevie B., the clown around town. Sure, we're buddies. But we don't see that much of each other. I'm usually going to auditions or to acting and dancing classes."

Bess was obviously relieved as Sally said, "Ellen, tell Bess and Nancy about some of your audition experiences."

"Just as soon as I call my voice mail," Ellen said. "Gotta see if I've got any callbacks."

Ellen returned to the table as they were digging into their salads. When the dessert menus arrived, Ellen suddenly excused herself. "I'd love to stuff down some decadent chocolate cake," she said, "but there was a message on my voice mail. I have to prepare for an audition on Monday, and I won't get much of a chance later this weekend. See you tomorrow, though."

After she left, Bess announced that she wouldn't mind skipping dessert, either. Sally then admitted that she'd filled up on the homemade rolls, so dessert was definitely out for her.

"Up to you, Nan," Bess said. "We'll watch."

"And nibble?" Nancy asked.

"Only if you insist," Sally answered.

Nancy ordered a chocolate mousse cheesecake and three forks, and they all dug in happily.

"It's almost ten. How about we call it a night?" Sally said after they had all licked their forks clean. "I want you two fresh for tomorrow's skating date."

"Are you letting me have the day off?" Nancy asked, pretending surprise. "Or am I supposed to solve the case tonight?"

"You're not going to hold that against me, forever, are you?" Sally asked.

"You can still make it up to me," Nancy said.

"How?" Sally asked warily.

"Get this restaurant to name a salad after me. Nancy's Noodles sounds good."

"Tell you what I *can* do," Sally said. "Treat you to a cab home."

"Deal." Nancy shook her friend's hand.

Sally dropped them in front of their apartment. As Nancy and Bess descended the steps to their entrance, Bess said, "It's awfully dark."

Nancy drew her key from her purse. "Didn't we leave an outside light on?"

Abruptly Bess gasped and grabbed Nancy's arm. "Don't tell me you saw another hat," Nancy teased.

Bess shouted her answer. "Look!" she said. A knife was sticking into the front door, anchoring a piece of paper.

Nancy quickly glanced around but saw and heard no one. After inserting her key, she slowly opened the door, listened a moment, then turned on a lamp before moving back to the open door.

Pinned under the knife was a page ripped from a magazine. Someone had printed over it with a heavy black marker. The large capital letters read: Drop your investigation before someone gets hurt!

Chapter

Six

NANCY TUGGED THE KNIFE LOOSE after wrapping the handle with a tissue from her purse. "Our first clue," she said dryly. It was an ordinary carving knife with a black plastic handle. "Though whoever left it probably didn't leave any fingerprints."

"Okay, drop it in." Bess shuddered, holding open a plastic bag she'd brought from the kitchen.

Nancy put the knife in the bag. Once inside, she laid the bag gently on the walnut coffee table. Then she studied the magazine page. The warning was printed right over the column "Our Best Guesses."

Nancy tapped the magazine page. "Let me think for a moment," she said, joining Bess on a sofa. "Aleta stands to lose her job if Rudolph's story line continues, and Joe stands to advance his career if the story line he wrote replaces the current one."

"That would also help his girlfriend's career," Bess added. "You know, Nan, they both had time to stick that knife in our door."

"If they knew where we were staying," said Nancy. "And something else, Bess," Nancy added reluctantly. "Remember that guy who followed us today?" Bess nodded. "I saw him in the restaurant," Nancy continued. "Just for a moment."

"Do you think he was following us again?" Bess asked, her eyes widening.

"No," Nancy replied. "He didn't seem to notice us, but he did take a long look at Aleta."

"I wonder if there's any connection," Bess said curiously.

Nancy became thoughtful. "It seems the only place to find answers is at the studio. We could use our ID key cards to get back in tonight."

"Suppose someone sees us sneaking around," Bess countered.

Nancy smiled. "I'm a consultant, right? So I left my consulting notes there."

Bess was dubious, but she put her coat back on. "We're not taking the subway, are we?"

"I think a cab is better at this hour," Nancy acknowledged.

During the ride over, Nancy explained to Bess

that she wasn't sure what they'd find in the offices. "But perhaps we'll get lucky and come across an issue of *Soap Talk* missing the page that was nailed to our door," she commented hopefully. She didn't want to mention that whoever sent them that warning might also be at the studio.

From behind his counter the night security guard glanced at their ID key cards, then gave them a ledger to sign in. A few names were already scrawled there, but the last two riveted Nancy's attention: Aleta McCloud and Joe Ortega. After signing in, Nancy inserted her key card into the heavy door separating the reception area from the studio. The lock clicked and the two girls opened the door.

As Nancy and Bess glanced cautiously down a long corridor, Bess asked softly, "Sally didn't say anything about taping a show tonight, so what are Aleta and Joe doing here?"

"Good question, Bess," Nancy said.

"I've got another one," Bess whispered. "Where are they?"

"Let's not worry about that now," Nancy responded. "Let's just hope we see them before they see us."

They used their key card to open Rochelle's office door, which was the nearest one. They gently closed the door behind them and turned on the light. Everything looked pretty much as they remembered, except that Rochelle had apparently cleaned off her desk before leaving for the day. "Should we look in her desk drawers and files?" Bess asked, still whispering.

"If we can get into them," Nancy replied. "But I imagine they're locked."

"No scripts lying around, either," Bess pointed out. "I guess they're being extra careful." As Bess turned toward the door, her sleeve caught the silver-framed photo on the credenza, knocking it to the floor. She gave a little yelp, then froze. "I hope no one heard that," she whispered, her face drained of color.

Nancy picked up the photo. "I doubt it, with the door shut." She checked the frame for any damage, then added, "Anyway, Bess, the frame's okay, so don't worry." Nancy studied the picture a moment longer before putting it back in place. "It's really a cute picture of a New York scene. A horse-drawn carriage and city bus all on the same busy street."

Nancy and Bess left the office and cautiously continued down the corridor to the office next to Rochelle's. The name on the door read Zack Mitchell, Music Coordinator.

"Isn't that the name Sally——" Nancy began.

Bess didn't let her finish. "It's that gorgeous blond guy we saw leaving the studio!" Bess put in.

Nancy grinned. "I should've known you'd remember." She used the key card to open the door. They heard a man's voice speaking in the dark. Bess grabbed Nancy's arm. The two girls stood frozen in the doorway.

Nancy's heart pounded as she waited for the man's reaction. But as the voice continued speaking, she calmed down enough to realize there was something odd about the words and tone. Then she heard, "So when you get this message, call me back in the morning."

Nancy patted Bess's hand, which was still clinging to her arm. "That's his answering machine," Nancy said reassuringly. "Someone was obviously leaving a message when we walked in."

"I was scared stiff," Bess said in a shaky voice.

"Me, too," Nancy admitted. "I was wondering how I'd explain looking for my notes in the music coordinator's office."

Bess laughed softly as she switched on the light. Nancy noticed a cassette and CD player in one corner of the room. The shelves above it were filled with audiotapes and CD's. Another table held a small computer. Loose sheets of music were scattered on the desk, but there were no issues of *Soap Talk* around.

Nancy and Bess left the office and continued on down the corridor. Joe's office was next, but before they could put the key card in the door, they heard faint voices in the distance. They stopped, listening intently.

Finally Bess whispered, "Aleta and Joe?"

"Let's see," Nancy whispered back. The thick carpeting masked the sounds of their steps as they moved toward a wedge of light coming from a partially opened office door. Suddenly Nancy put out her arm, bringing Bess to a halt. They were close enough to hear distinct words.

One of the voices was Aleta's. Another was of a woman whom Aleta called "Yvonne." Soon Joe's voice joined in.

"You'll have to memorize these lines, Aleta," Joe was saying. "If Gardiner orders Karl to dump his story line, we have to be ready to go with this one. You ready, Yvonne?"

"I've already made notes for blocking the scene," the other woman replied.

A second male voice broke in. "Do I step in front of Aleta or push her out of the way?"

Nancy's eyes widened, but Bess gave a loud gasp as they recognized Steve Basset's voice. Suddenly the corridor was flooded with light as the door opened all the way. Joe stepped out and locked eyes with Nancy. She managed a smile, despite the sinking sensation in her stomach.

Joe didn't return her smile. "What are you doing here?" he demanded.

"We're looking for Mr. Gardiner's office," Nancy said, thinking quickly.

By now Aleta, Steve, and a very attractive woman with jet-black hair had come into the corridor. They all seemed to be upset. Nancy knew they would not want anyone—particularly Karl—to find out they were rehearsing a new story line behind his back.

"What do you want?" Aleta asked coldly.

"I forgot my notes—for the teenage-runaway story," Nancy said calmly. "Mr. Gardiner said I could come over and get them."

"On the first floor?" Joe said, still unsmiling. "His office is on the third floor."

Nancy didn't lose her cool. "We heard voices and thought it might be Mr. Gardiner talking with someone."

"I don't think we've met," the dark-haired woman said, crossing her arms over her red leather minidress. Her eyes were narrowed with suspicion, and she tapped a black, over-the-knee boot on the floor.

"Then you're in for a treat," Steve said quickly. "Yvonne, these two fair ladies are consulting with Karl about a new story line. Nancy Drew, Bess Marvin, meet Yvonne De Young, a brilliant director."

Yvonne smiled sardonically as they all shook hands, though Nancy noticed that the woman was watching her intently. "A teenage-runaway story. I don't believe I've heard much about that."

Joe's voice dripped with sarcasm. "Everything's top secret now, Yvonne, or hadn't you noticed?" He turned back to Nancy. "So, how much did you hear while you were eavesdropping?"

Nancy stared into four pairs of suspicious eyes. "We heard something about a scene to replace the one in which Laura gets murdered," she said evenly.

Joe remained silent, gazing down at the floor intently.

"You're in this scene, too, Steve?" Bess interjected.

"I'm the one who saves Laura," Steve volunteered. "It gives me either a career boost—or a career boot, depending on Karl's reaction if he hears about it."

"He won't hear about it from us," Bess said warmly. "And if they take you and Laura off the show, I won't watch it anymore," she added loyally.

"I hope you find your notes," Joe said sarcastically.

Nancy didn't care. She was more intent now on just getting out of there. "I'm pretty sure I left them in Mr. Gardiner's office," she said.

Steve pointed to a stairway sign. "You can take those stairs up to the third floor." He turned back to the others. "Come on, Joe, let's finish up. I need my beauty sleep for tomorrow." He winked at Bess. "See you girls then."

Nancy and Bess hurried up the stairs, then took the elevator back down to the main floor. Once outside, they hailed a passing cab.

"Let's call it a night, huh, Nan?" Bess said, sitting back with a *whoosh* of relief.

"Fine with me," Nancy replied. "We need to rest up for tomorrow. Apparently, Steve's looking forward to it, too."

Bess frowned. "Maybe because his *friend* Ellen is coming, too."

"I don't think you have anything to worry about," Nancy said.

"How about the note on our door?" Bess asked. "Should we be worrying about that?"

"Well," Nancy said slowly. "If any of the four people tonight were responsible for that warning, they'll be even more suspicious after seeing us at the studio."

"But we didn't find out anything," Bess said.

"They might think we did," Nancy responded. Silently she wondered how long the person would wait to make good on the threat.

Sally called in the morning, asking Nancy and Bess to meet her to rent skates, helmets, and knee and elbow pads.

Steve, Ellen, and Sally were already at the rental place talking to a tall guy with white-blond hair.

"Doesn't he look like the guy we saw yesterday, Nan?" Bess asked. "I wonder if he's Ellen's boyfriend."

Nancy knew Bess was just trying to make sure Steve was available. Ellen introduced the handsome newcomer as Zack Mitchell, the music coordinator on *Love and Loss*.

"Have you done much skating?" Zack asked, his unexpectedly dark brown eyes hypnotizing Nancy.

"Not too much," Nancy said. She felt her face getting hot. The way Zack was looking at her made it plain that he wasn't anyone else's date. Steve, meanwhile, had made a beeline for Bess, solving that problem.

Ellen suggested they all head across the park toward Sheep Meadow. She thought the views were prettiest along that route. "I'd better keep an eye on you, then," Zack said, taking Nancy's arm. "It gets kind of tricky skating in the park with all the traffic."

"Traffic?" Nancy found it hard to concentrate with Zack so close.

Zack chuckled. "I don't mean cars. But on a warm spring day everybody's out and feeling a little wild. Kids on tricycles, adults on bicycles, first-time skaters—you have to stay alert."

Nancy didn't feel very alert with Zack's strong warm hand on her arm. In fact, she felt somewhat dazed. The group finally stopped at a park bench to put on the skates and protective gear. Zack insisted on making sure Nancy's helmet fit right, tightening the strap under her chin. Don't get carried away, she told herself, conjuring up her boyfriend Ned Nickerson's image through a haze of guilt. Then Bess caught her eye and winked before skating off with Steve. Nancy winked back, and then she and Zack took off after them.

Nancy always found it amazing that such a huge expanse of green park existed in the heart of a city known for its skyscrapers.

"On summer nights they have concerts in the park," Zack said. "I think they're worth coming back for. Don't you? There's nothing like listening to music under the stars—with someone special."

He smiled, and Nancy had to smile back. Then she tore her eyes away from his, telling herself she'd better look where she was going, in more ways than one. Up ahead she noticed a small pond with a quaint little stone bridge. It looked like a charming old-fashioned picture from a child's nursery-rhyme book.

She realized her speed was picking up a bit because the path sloped downward toward the pond. Zack must have noticed it, too, because she suddenly heard him say, "Watch yourself, Nan."

By this time the others were already past the pond and the small footbridge. Sally turned to wave at Nancy and Zack. Suddenly she froze, her mouth open as if to scream. Nancy had almost reached the beginning of the bridge, but before she could react to her friend's odd behavior, she felt something cold and hard smash into the backs of her legs. The momentum pushed her forward, and she reached out towards the railing that skirted the pond, trying to steady herself. But it was too low. She pitched forward, helplessly aware that she was plunging headfirst onto the rocks lining the pond below.

Chapter

Seven

NANCY'S BLOOD RAN COLD as she realized what was happening to her. Just as she was about to plunge headfirst onto a jagged rock, she felt herself being jerked upward. Her jacket pulled tight against her chest as Zack grabbed it from behind to stop her fall. Nancy thrust her left arm back and made a grab for the railing to steady herself.

In seconds Nancy was safely upright, even though her legs were shaky and her heart was thudding in her chest.

"Wow," Nancy said, pushing her hair out of her eyes. "That was too close."

Zack gaped at a grocery cart loaded with odds and ends resting at the foot of the bridge. "How could an accident like this happen?" he asked as he slipped a comforting arm around Nancy's shoulders.

Nancy leaned back against him and glanced around. "Maybe it wasn't an accident," she responded.

At that exact moment Steve came racing over the bridge, followed closely by the others. "I saw the whole thing," he said breathlessly. "Someone deliberately shoved that cart at you. It came from over there." They all turned and saw someone in a dark running suit, the hood pulled up, running from the deep shadows. Glancing back in their direction, the runner picked up speed.

"Hey, you!" Steve shouted at the runner, taking off in quick pursuit.

The runner ran along a footpath toward the open expanse of Sheep Meadow. Steve's in-line skates almost gave him the speed to catch up. But once the runner reached the grass lawn and started across the field, Steve's skates prevented him from following. Outmaneuvered, he headed back to join the others.

The group had gathered around a large gray rock near the foot of the bridge. "Look at this," he said, holding out a worn overcoat. "I found it in the shadows by the bench."

"Looks like the runner was pretending to be a street person," Nancy commented.

"And waited for an opportunity to push the cart at Nancy," Bess added.

"But why would a runner do that?" Sally asked, puzzled.

"Could be some sort of crazy vendetta toward skaters," Zack commented, his bright blue eyes fixed on Nancy. "Some runners feel that skaters are a hazard and should be restricted to certain areas of the park."

"Seems to me the park's big enough for everyone," Ellen said.

"Did you get a look at the runner, Steve?" Nancy asked hopefully.

"No. I couldn't make out much of the face. Whoever it was was wearing wraparound sunglasses with the hood drawn tight."

"That means it could have been a woman," Nancy said. "I say we take a look at the stuff in the cart. There might be a clue," she added, eager to find out more.

At first glance the contents of the grocery cart didn't appear to contain any clues. Jumbled together were odds and ends of clothing and boxes. But suddenly a familiar magazine cover caught Nancy's attention. Plucking it out, she saw that it was a copy of *Soap Talk* with a hand-printed message on the cover: I warned you someone could get hurt. Drop it!

"What is it?" Bess inquired. "A clue?" Before Nancy could respond, Bess snatched up the magazine. "This is going too far," Bess remarked excitedly.

"You're right," Sally agreed, peering at the

message from over Bess's shoulder. "Nancy, don't put yourself in any more danger. Tell Peter Gardiner the deal's off."

Zack glanced at Nancy curiously. "Why don't you tell the rest of us what's going on?" he asked her.

Nancy hesitated and then realized that her cover had been blown anyway. So she explained that she had agreed to investigate the source of the story leaks.

"Then whoever is leaking the story line obviously knows you're investigating this for Gardiner," Steve said. "But how?"

"I don't know," Nancy said soberly. "All I know is that someone is trying to warn me off this case."

"What will you do?" Ellen asked, concerned.

"For now, relax and have fun," Nancy said, smiling at Zack. "After all, that's the real reason I'm in New York."

"Sounds terrific," Bess declared. "But the only thing I want to do now is take off these skates. My feet are killing me."

"You'll feel better after you have something to eat," Steve said. "Let me treat you all to lunch. I know just the spot."

The group skated back to the rental shop. After returning their gear, they walked along Central Park South toward the Plaza Hotel. They crossed a small square with thousands of red and yellow tulips in bloom, and then Steve escorted them toward the entrance to the Plaza Hotel.

Nancy thought the hotel resembled a palace, with uniformed attendants opening doors to a continuous line of limousines.

"Okay, guys," Steve said with a grin, "we're here." He stopped at a waiting stretch limousine and opened the back door. "Step in."

Overcome by Steve's boldness, the girls froze with embarrassment.

"It's cool, really," Zack said reassuringly. "We arranged for a limo to meet us here."

"Meals on the move," Steve said, bowing. He waved them inside with a flourish. "Your table awaits." Turning to Zack, he said, "Take over for me, pal. I'll be back in a jiff."

Steve soon returned, balancing a stack of steaming hot dogs on top of a six-pack of cold sodas. "There's nothing like a New York street vendor's hot dog," he declared as the limo started down the street.

"Yum, they smell delicious," Nancy commented. Then glancing around the plush interior, she added, "This is what I call a hot dog with the works."

"Nancy and Bess should visit New York more often," Ellen said. "The guys never spoiled us like this before. And what else have you two cooked up for us? Are we going somewhere special?"

"How about a night on the town?" Zack asked. "If you're all up to it, we could stop at the Side Pocket to shoot pool, then have dinner."

"Let's!" Bess exclaimed, her blue eyes sparkling.

Sally looked at Ellen, who nodded readily. "We're game," she said.

"Sounds great. I'm up for anything," Nancy agreed, smiling at Zack. "Just give us time to freshen up."

They all decided to meet at the B and B in a few hours. After everyone had finished lunch, the limo drove Nancy and Bess home first.

Several hours later Zack and Steve rang their doorbell and escorted the two girls to a waiting cab. Sally and Ellen were to meet the group at the pool hall. Peering out the window as they rode along, Nancy thought that New York by night was even more exciting than by day. She noticed dozens of people strolling the sidewalks, stopping to watch street performers or admiring displays in shop windows.

"Here we are," Zack announced. They climbed out in front of an old brick factory that had been converted into a billiard club.

The Side Pocket certainly looked lively, Nancy thought. Each window was outlined in neon, and the door handles were made from real cue sticks. Inside, there were people everywhere—sleek women in designer outfits and men in silk shirts and jeans.

"Come on, guys," Sally said eagerly as she and Ellen joined the group. "Let's hit the tables!"

Nancy thought that Sally looked terrific in a red turtleneck and jeans, with silver and bead earrings that almost reached her shoulders.

The group found an empty table in the back. Bess and Steve announced that they were content to sit and watch the others play.

Zack's muscular arms made quick work of racking the balls. "Will you do the honors?" he asked, handing Sally a cue stick.

The bright light over the pool table highlighted the contrast between Zack's white-blond hair and dark brown eyes. Sally broke, sending the balls scattering to all parts of the table. Zack and Ellen took their turns. Then Nancy was next.

"The two ball into the corner pocket," Nancy announced. She carefully lined up her shot, then hit the cue ball in the exact right spot.

"Wow! That was some shot," Zack remarked, chalking up the tip of his cue stick.

Just then Nancy's blue eyes widened as she spotted someone across the room. Her spine tingled. "Look over there," she said to Zack, pointing discreetly. "The short stocky man with the mustache. He followed Bess and me yesterday, and he was at the restaurant last night."

The man's eyes locked once again on Nancy's.

He seemed to be studying her in a cold, detached way.

"Isn't that what's-his-name, the soap columnist?" Steve asked.

"Yeah, that's Conover," Sally confirmed angrily. "He's the one who prints the story leaks in his column. I feel like giving him a piece of my mind. He's nothing but a troublemaker."

"Sally's right, he's trouble," Steve said sternly. "I say we split. I don't want to be seen in the same place with him. It's too easy to become a victim of guilt by association. I'm on thin ice with Rudolph as it is."

"You're right, we should leave here now," Ellen said nervously. "Zack and Sally shouldn't take any risks, either."

Nancy couldn't help but wonder whether they were overreacting. For a moment Nancy considered questioning Conover, but then decided the time wasn't right. At least, Nancy thought as they were leaving, I know who followed us yesterday, though I still need to find out why.

Once outside, the group strolled to a cozy French café. Nancy and Bess split a bouillabaisse, while the others enjoyed a variety of beef and lamb specialties. Afterward they chatted about show business over coffee.

"I got hooked on acting when I was about nine," Ellen said, her green eyes sparkling. "My mother took me to see *Dance Dance Dance* on

Broadway. After that, all I ever wanted to be was an actress."

"My father took me to that show, too," Nancy said. "When we visited my aunt Eloise. You and I probably saw it around the same time—with different reactions." She laughed. "I didn't want to be an actress."

"Just as well," Ellen said with a grin. "I don't need any more competition."

"Maybe Sally can help you get another part on *Love and Loss,*" Bess suggested.

"I would if I could," Sally said. "But once an actor or actress has been a day-player on the show, his or her name drops to the bottom of the casting list, which prevents the audience from recognizing any particular day-player."

"Illusion is part of showbiz magic," Steve put in. "If a day-player is spotted too often in different roles the illusion of the show can be blown."

Zack glanced at his watch. "It's still early, guys. Why don't we pop over to the Jazz Note for a few sets?"

"I think I'll pass," Sally said with a yawn, covering her mouth with her hand. "I'm beat."

"Me, too," Ellen said. "And I have to get up early to practice for my audition on Monday."

Bess flashed Nancy a pleading look across the table. "Guess the guys are stuck with us," Nancy said with a smile, picking up on Bess's signal.

After putting Sally and Ellen into taxis, the

foursome walked a short distance to Washington Square, the heart of Greenwich Village. In the center of the park they stopped to admire the large stone arch. Even in the evening light it was impressive. They continued walking and soon reached the art-deco entrance to the jazz club. Zack gave the number of their party to a man standing at the door, and the group was quickly ushered to a tiny table in the main room.

Nancy blinked in amazement at the room, which looked as if it were straight out of the 1930s. The walls were covered with dark wood paneling, and the only light came from the art-deco wall sconces and a lit-up glass panel behind the musicians.

"This is great!" Nancy said enthusiastically. The music was pulsing through the club, and Nancy couldn't resist tapping her foot to the beat.

Zack exchanged a grin with Nancy, obviously pleased by her reaction. "I thought if I could make New York attractive enough to you, you'd want to come back."

Wondering why his dark eyes made her feel tongue-tied, Nancy finally said, "I've always liked New York. But it's especially great this time."

After listening to a few sets of music, the foursome finally decided to call an end to their day.

"What a day!" Bess remarked happily. "What

a night, too! I've had a fabulous time, Steve, thanks to you."

Steve looked genuinely pleased as he took Bess's hand in his and raised it to his lips and kissed it.

Bess's eyes shone with delight. Steve Basset had actually kissed her.

By the time Nancy and Bess returned to the apartment, they were both eager to get some sleep. Nancy went into the bathroom to wash up.

"Looks like Zack has a crush on you, Nan," Bess said, slipping out of her clothes and into a nightshirt.

Nancy felt a bit guilty because of Ned. "He's a nice guy," she said quickly, splashing water on her face.

"And a hunk," Bess added.

"He is cute," Nancy agreed. "But don't get any ideas." She dried her face, then went back into the bedroom.

Suddenly the phone rang. Nancy moved to answer it. "It's probably Sally wanting the scoop on the rest of our evening," Bess said.

Nancy picked up the receiver. "Hello? Oh—no!" Her expression grew serious as she jotted an address on a slip of paper. "We'll meet you right away." Nancy hung up and turned to Bess.

"That was Peter Gardiner," Nancy said. "He wants us to meet him as soon as possible. Karl Rudolph has been murdered!"

Chapter

Eight

MURDERED!" BESS EXCLAIMED. "I can't believe it. What happened?"

"Peter didn't say," Nancy responded. "We're to meet him at Karl Rudolph's brownstone as soon as possible. He'll fill us in on the details there."

Their taxi pulled up along a row of double-parked squad cars in front of Rudolph's Upper West Side brownstone. Nancy and Bess got out and walked over to where Gardiner was being interviewed by a police detective.

"You have no idea why the deceased telephoned you earlier?" the young, curly-haired detective asked.

"No. I was out to dinner," Gardiner answered soberly. "When I returned home there was a message from Rudolph on my answering machine to call him. He said there was something he needed to discuss, but when I called, you answered the phone, Detective, and asked me to meet you here."

"Was it unusual for Rudolph to call you at home?" the detective inquired.

"Not at all. He often called to run a story idea by me," Gardiner responded. Then he turned to Nancy and Bess. "Oh, good—you're here. This is Detective Asher. I know you'll want to speak to him."

"There's no statement for the press at this time," said the detective with a wave of his hand.

"We're not reporters," Nancy replied. "I'm Nancy Drew and this is my associate, Bess Marvin."

"Ms. Drew is a detective," Gardiner explained.

"Why'd you send for her?" Asher asked.

"She's been helping me out with a little problem on the show," Gardiner said.

"And what's this problem that caused you to contact a detective?" Asher asked.

"One of our major story lines was leaked to the press," Gardiner began. Soon he'd told the whole story. The detective listened carefully without taking notes.

"I see," Asher said finally. "Anything you can add, Ms. Drew?"

"Only that Karl Rudolph was determined to

find the source of the leaks," Nancy told him, deciding not to mention the warning notes for now.

"Well, it looks like you've come here for nothing," Asher concluded. "The evidence points to homicide during a burglary. If the three of you care to go inside, you'll see for yourselves. The body has been removed."

Asher led them inside, and Nancy took in the living room. Karl Rudolph's home resembled his office at Premiere Broadcasting. Stacks of scripts were piled precariously on tables; rows of books and videotapes were packed into bookshelves; and in an adjoining study, papers covered the entire surface of a mahogany desk.

After a quick tour of the crime scene by Asher, Nancy had several questions. "Who discovered the body and called the police?" she asked him.

"An employee of the security company that monitors the building's alarm system," Asher replied.

"And how did the murderer get inside?" Nancy inquired.

"We're working on that," the detective said. "There don't appear to be signs of forced entry."

"You're losing me," Bess murmured. "Didn't you just tell us someone from the security company found the body? Why would someone come here if the alarm wasn't set off by a break-in?"

"It seems that Rudolph's security system is fairly sophisticated," Asher explained. "It's programmed to alert the security company if it's not set by a certain time each night. They follow up with a phone call to the residence, and if there's no answer, they send someone to check things out. Apparently, that's what happened tonight."

"How do you explain a burglar entering without breaking in?" Nancy asked pointedly.

"Well, I really can't explain it," Asher responded, rubbing one hand through his dark, curly hair. "But I've got a couple of theories. First, that Rudolph let the burglar in on some pretext." Watching Nancy's reaction, Asher continued. "Another possibility is that the burglar was lurking nearby. When Rudolph put the trash out, he set himself up to be robbed."

"And murdered," Gardiner added grimly.

"Unfortunately," Asher said with a frown. "My guess is that the burglar forced Rudolph to let him in."

"I'm not sure," Nancy said slowly, pushing a strand of her reddish blond hair behind one ear. "Something seems wrong to me. It's too easy."

"Easy?" Asher put in, surprised. "What's easy about this, Ms. Drew?"

"It would be easy for the killer to fake a burglary that would cover up any other reason the killer had for being in the house."

Asher hesitated for a moment. "I like the way your mind works. But we've got to go on facts, not theories. And the facts point to burglary." Asher puffed up his cheeks and let out a sigh.

"Mr. Gardiner confirmed that Rudolph wore a gold watch and a diamond ring. They're missing, along with the cash from his wallet."

"Is anything else missing?" Nancy asked.

"We'll check with the insurance inventory tomorrow," Asher said, handing Nancy his card. "Please call me if you have any more thoughts. Right now I need to get to the station and fill out a report."

"One more thing," Nancy asked. "How was Rudolph killed?"

"A blow to the head," Asher responded. "And the killer didn't leave the murder weapon behind."

Everyone filed outside. On the sidewalk Peter Gardiner told Nancy that he accepted the burglary theory. "There's nothing illegal about passing our story line to the press," Gardiner said. "So I doubt anyone would get involved in murder over it."

If burglary was the motive, why was so little taken? Nancy thought. Surely there were more valuables in the house.

By the time Nancy and Bess returned to the bed-and-breakfast, they were both exhausted. Nevertheless, Nancy had trouble falling asleep. There were too many unanswered questions whirling in her head. And she still didn't have the slightest idea why anyone was leaking the show's story line.

The morning sun came too soon when Nancy realized she'd slept for only a few hours. Raising her head, she yawned and looked out the window. It was a glorious spring morning. "Are you up, Bess?" Nancy asked.

Bess mumbled, burying her head under the pillow.

Nancy reached for her purse on the nightstand. Then she took out Detective Asher's card and dialed his number. He answered himself. "I have a few more questions," Nancy told him. "It would help me to see Rudolph's brownstone again. I know you're busy, but could we meet there in a little while?"

Asher said he'd see her there in an hour. The girls dressed quickly, leaving enough time to stop for muffins and coffee.

As the girls approached Rudolph's brownstone, Nancy noted the trash cans near the entrance to the street level. Like Detective Asher, she thought that someone could hide under the stairs up to the first floor unnoticed. Still a hazy thought kept nagging at her.

"Just as I thought," Nancy said as she checked the area outside the street-level entrance. "There's no sign of a struggle."

Bess gazed at Nancy in amazement. "Okay, Nan. Tell me why you think that."

"Rudolph was a big man. He couldn't easily be forced back into his house. Now look at the door,

Bess," she continued. "There's an even layer of soot on it. If someone tried to force the door open, the soot would be smeared from pressing against it."

"Then Karl Rudolph must have let his murderer in," Bess responded. "Which means he probably knew him. Or her."

Nancy and Bess took the stone stairs up to the first-floor entrance. An officer in civilian clothes led them to the study, where Asher waited by a window.

"Find anything of interest outside?" he asked, looking at Nancy.

"Not really," Nancy fibbed. She decided to wait until she had more evidence to tell him her findings. "Do you mind if we check out the desk?"

"Help yourselves. I know you'll be careful," Asher replied as he left the room.

"What exactly are we looking for, Nan?" Bess asked, lifting a stack of papers.

Nancy frowned. "Well, for one thing, a clue to link the murder to the story leaks. It's a long shot, but you never know."

Nancy spotted an old high school yearbook lying open and upside down. Picking it up, she noticed a large manila envelope underneath. Inside were some yellowing typewritten pages. The first page read *"The Evil Twin,* a play by Karl Rudolph, for the School of the Performing Arts."

Anything for Love

"What're you staring at?" Bess asked.

Nancy held up the envelope. "Here's a play he wrote in high school and his yearbook."

"What're they doing on his desk?"

"Maybe he was planning to use part of his old play in one of his new story lines," Nancy replied.

Bess shrugged. "Looks like Karl Rudolph didn't throw anything away."

Nancy nodded. Then she noticed the phone on a corner of the desk. "The phone has a redial button," she said. "Maybe we can find out who Rudolph called last."

Nancy took a pen and small notepad from her purse before lifting the receiver to her ear. She pressed the button. "It's ringing."

"Hello!" came a recording on the other end. It was a familiar woman's voice. "You've reached five five five four seven four two." Nancy quickly jotted down the number.

"Who was it?" Bess asked curiously.

"An answering machine," Nancy said, "but I got the number. The voice sounded familiar, but I can't place it."

The two girls joined Asher in the living room. "Nice piece of detective work, Ms. Drew," Asher said as Nancy showed him the information. "Seems we missed that one. Let's go back to the phone for a moment."

Asher moved into the study and picked up the

81

phone. He entered the number for address verification and identified himself to the operator along with the number to be verified.

"That number is issued to Rochelle Foster," Nancy could hear the operator inform him. "Three ten East Ninety-first Street."

Chapter

Nine

WHO IS ROCHELLE FOSTER?" Detective Asher asked.

"The casting director on the show," Nancy replied.

Asher took out his notes. "Would it be unusual for him to call her?"

Nancy shook her head. "Not necessarily."

Asher made a note. "I'll check it out."

"Look," Nancy said, pointing to Rudolph's VCR. "The machine is on."

Asher nodded. "There's no tape in it. Evidently, when Rudolph finished watching, he didn't turn off the machine."

Nancy checked out the room, until her eyes lighted on a bookcase filled with videotapes. She walked over to it. "You think he put the tape back?" Nancy asked.

"Yes—or it was stolen. The burglars seemed to prefer the small stuff. They didn't go after TVs, the VCR, or the microwave."

Nancy pulled a stool over and climbed up on it to get a better look at the stack of videotapes. Each was labeled with a number. One cover near the top of a stack seemed out of line.

"What is it?" Asher asked.

"One tape is missing. There's a number 5733 and a number 5735. But no 5734." Nancy remembered Rudolph's office. It looked like a mess, but the man said he could find anything he needed quickly. And all the other tapes were in order. "Would it be possible for me to check Rudolph's office at work?" Nancy asked Asher. "There might be something in it that could give us a lead."

"Well . . ." Asher began reluctantly. "It's been sealed off, and we've already checked it out thoroughly. There was no tape."

Nancy smiled, not wanting to antagonize him, and climbed down from the stool to take one last look around. She was struck by a small spotlight in the ceiling that seemed to be focused on the fireplace mantel. On the mantel, she noticed a clean circle outlined by a thin film of dust.

Asher, sounding a bit defensive, said, "If you're looking at the circle, we saw it, too.

Apparently, an art object of some kind was displayed there. We'll be getting an inventory from Rudolph's friends and a list of valuables from his insurance company."

"I'm sure you've been very thorough," Nancy said reassuringly. She didn't want him to feel uncomfortable. She started to turn away from the fireplace when something on the fire screen caught her eye. As she bent over, Asher said, "Nothing gets by you, does it?"

"Or you," Nancy said, matching his wry and playful tone. "I take it these are strands of hair?"

"Right. Red hair. We'll be doing an analysis to see whether any of our known criminals match up."

Bess exchanged a glance with Nancy, but the girls said nothing until they were outside.

Then Bess said, "I can't believe Aleta would kill him. Though she did say her hair has been falling out from stress."

"If it's Aleta's hair, it puts her at the scene," Nancy said. "But not necessarily last night." Then she added, "Five seven three four. Let's find a phone, Bess, before I forget that tape number. I'm betting it's an episode of *Love and Loss.*"

At a public phone booth in the next block, Nancy phoned Gardiner. "That is an old number for the show," he confirmed. "Well over a year ago." He explained that the old tapes were stored in the basement of the studio, along with copies of the scripts. And, yes, Nancy's ID key card would get her in.

Nancy filled Bess in on her talk with Gardiner, adding, "But there's no sense dragging you along—"

"Yes, there is," Bess interrupted firmly.

"Bess, I'm just going to see if the tape is there. If Rudolph's copy was stolen, there might be something on it that's important to the thief. There's really no reason for you to come, too. It'll probably be a waste of time. Why don't you get us theater tickets for that new show, *Love Notes*? I hear the revival of *Seven Sisters* is great, too."

Bess folded her arms. "I'm not letting you go anywhere alone, Nan."

Nancy put an arm around her friend's shoulders. "Look," she said, "I appreciate your concern. But there's no danger lurking in a storage room on a Sunday morning. In the meantime, if you stand in line at the ticket booth, we'll have a shot at some good seats for tonight."

Bess hesitated. "You're sure that's all you're going to do? Look for the tape?"

"I'm sure." They agreed on a time to meet back at the apartment and both took off.

At the studio a different guard passed her the sign-in ledger. She asked the man directions to the basement, and he barely looked up from the magazine he was reading to point her toward the right door.

Nancy quickly made her way down one long flight of stairs and into a huge room running the length and width of the studio building. The walls and floors were cement. Some pipes, part of the heating and sprinkler system, crisscrossed the ceiling. As far as Nancy could see, the room was filled with row upon row of metal shelving stacked from floor to ceiling with labeled cartons. There was barely enough room to walk between the narrow aisles separating the steel shelves.

Nancy checked the numbers of the cartons near the entrance. They were in the hundreds, which meant the larger numbers had to be toward the back. She squeezed down one aisle that ran from front to back, until she came to the five thousands. Then she turned down that aisle until she came to a carton marked 5700. She slowed down. Each carton held twenty tapes, which meant the one she wanted should be two cartons below. Nancy counted down, then bent over to check a carton on the lowest shelf. That should be the one. She had just pulled it out when she suddenly heard a horrible screeching noise. It sounded as if two heavy pieces of steel were crashing into each other. As she started to turn, the shelving behind her began to topple toward her. As it fell, the boxes on the shelves slid forward. Her heart pounding, Nancy realized she was trapped between two sections of steel shelving.

She pushed desperately against the boxes coming toward her, but there were too many of them. Unless she could get out of the aisle, the falling boxes would crush her. But there was no place to run. The aisles were already filled with fallen boxes. She started to scream but she realized no one would hear anything.

She instinctively bent over the box she had pulled out. But even if she had had time to empty it, it wasn't big enough to crawl inside. Then she heard the crash of steel as another stack of shelving closer to her fell against its neighbor. If she wasn't crushed by the cartons, the steel shelving would do the job. She crouched lower over the box, trying desperately to push away the thought that this time there was no way out. But the sounds of steel crashing against steel and boxes thudding against one another was almost overwhelming.

Chapter

Ten

THINK, NANCY, THINK! she told herself desperately. Bending low over the box of tapes, she noticed an empty space on the shelf where the tape box had been. She quickly shoved the box out of her way and crawled onto the shelf, just as a heavy load of boxes crashed to the floor where she'd been standing moments before.

Hemmed in by boxes, Nancy expected the shelving she was crouched on to fall over, taking her with it. But to her intense relief, it remained standing. She carefully reached a hand behind her and touched cement. So that was it. The back wall was directly behind her and kept the shelving from falling.

Boxes continued to fall, until, finally, all was

quiet. Nancy extended her cramped leg, intending to push against the boxes blocking her, when suddenly she heard footsteps—and instantly froze. Those boxes didn't just happen to fall, she realized, and whoever had pushed them over was still out there. Then she heard a door open and slam shut.

Shaken, Nancy realized that the person who had left the room thought that his or her mission had been accomplished. Despite her cramped position, she decided to stay put a little longer, to make sure that whoever had gone wasn't coming back. After a few minutes she cautiously extended her foot until it touched one of the boxes blocking her way. To her relief, when she pressed harder, the box moved. She began shoving with both her feet and then her hands, finally clearing a small passage.

The boxes had not fallen evenly. Some were supporting others like makeshift scaffolding, creating small pockets of space. Nancy began squeezing through these. Above her, the shelving and boxes, jammed together, formed an odd canopy. She could even stand up in some places by kicking and lifting boxes out of the way.

Once she was sure no more boxes would come tumbling down, Nancy returned to her original shelving and dug through the debris to find the box she'd pulled out. It was at the very bottom, its numbers clearly visible.

She pried the top open and checked each tape

inside. They were all there, except 5734. She counted them to make sure. Nineteen. One short. Whoever had knocked the shelving over had taken the tape before she got there.

As she began pushing her way toward the door, Nancy suddenly remembered that Gardiner had mentioned that the scripts were also stored in the basement. That script might provide a lead, if it hadn't been taken, too. But where would it be kept? She turned back and wearily crawled over another pile of fallen boxes and shelving. Once clear of them, she glanced around to get her bearings. An entire group of shelving was still standing on the far side of the cement room. Happily she discovered that the boxes on the shelf contained scripts.

Naturally, the box she wanted would be at the bottom. With a sigh, she pulled the script out and glanced at the cover page to make sure. Yes, number 5734. As she was about to carry it off, one of the writers' names caught her eye: Luther De Young.

He had to be related to Yvonne. The cover page also listed the first names of the characters except for one listed simply as "nurse."

Nancy sat down on one of the boxes and fished through her purse until she found the list Sally had made for her. All the performers, directors, and writers were listed with addresses and phone numbers.

At a wall telephone next to the door she dialed

Yvonne's number. An answering machine said, "Luther and Yvonne cannot take your call right now." Nancy hung up and pondered for a moment. Most likely Luther was Yvonne's husband. But no one had mentioned his being a writer on the show.

Nancy consulted her list, noting Aleta's address and phone number. She thought that Aleta might be able to tell her more about Luther De Young. Nancy also wanted to see whether Aleta would admit to being at Rudolph's house the night before. Nancy hoped she'd catch her off guard. She dialed the phone, and Aleta answered. The actress didn't sound particularly surprised to hear from Nancy. Nancy considered the fact that Aleta lived close enough to be home by now, if she'd been the one who had stolen the tape and knocked over the shelving. "I'd like to talk to you about some things," Nancy said. "It won't take long."

Aleta was cool. "I'm sorry, I'm busy. Some other time."

"It concerns Rudolph," Nancy said. "I assume you know what happened."

She heard Aleta's quick intake of breath. "Yes, I heard. It's horrible. But I don't see how it concerns *me.*"

Nancy decided to take a chance. "Look, I know you visited Rudolph last night. I think it's best we speak first."

"First?" Aleta's voice almost squeaked.

Nancy smiled to herself. Her probe had paid off. Aleta hadn't denied being at Rudolph's. "The police will be calling you," Nancy continued.

"How do you know?" Aleta's hard tone had returned.

"I'd rather continue this conversation in person."

After a pause Aleta said, "I'll meet you at the studio, but let's be quick. I really am busy."

Nancy stopped in one of the ladies' rooms. One glance in the mirror told her she needed more than a quick brushing off. Her face and hands were streaked with dirt. Fortunately, she'd been wearing black denim jeans and a leather jacket. Her clothes cleaned up pretty well after a few swipes from a damp paper towel. She dampened a few more towels and washed her face, then combed her hair and put on some lipstick. She was fairly presentable.

She reached wardrobe before Aleta. Apparently, the actress was in no hurry to see Nancy. Racks of clothes filled the center of two rooms, while shelves of sweaters and accessories lined the walls. Each rack and shelf was labeled with an actor's name. Slips of paper with dates and scenes written on them were pinned to some of the outfits. As Nancy started to read a few, she heard a door open and Aleta's voice demanding, "Okay, I'm here. What do you want?"

Nancy turned. "Thanks for coming."

Aleta waved her hand contemptuously. "You caught me by surprise when you mentioned the police. I can't believe they think I was at Karl Rudolph's place. Because I wasn't."

Nancy let that go for the moment. Instead, she reached into her purse and pulled out the heavy script. "I see Luther De Young wrote this."

Aleta glanced at it, obviously neither surprised nor interested. "So?"

"No one told me he was writing for the show."

"He isn't," Aleta said flatly.

"Then why—"

Aleta broke in, clearly anxious to finish up the interview. "Luther used to be one of the writers. Yvonne got him his chance after she became a director here. But once she supported me for the role of Laura, Karl began criticizing Luther's scripts. He told Gardiner they needed too much editing. Gardiner had wanted to give Luther a chance, but when your head writer says he's unhappy—and your show is number one—well, he calls the shots. Luther was fired."

Nancy studied the young woman before her. Aleta certainly didn't seem very sorry about the man losing his job just because his wife had helped Aleta get hired. "Is that what you meant when you said Rudolph finds a way to get even eventually?" Nancy asked.

"That's one example. But are you suggesting

Luther had anything to do with Karl's death? Is that what the police think?"

"The police think that a burglar or burglars may have been lying in wait until Rudolph took out the trash," Nancy informed her.

Aleta shuddered. "It's hard to believe that I was—" She broke off, biting her lip.

Nancy finished it for her. "That you were visiting Rudolph when someone was hiding there?"

"I never said I was there," Aleta insisted. "I don't know why you keep implying that I was."

"Is your hair still falling out?" Nancy asked, as if changing the subject.

Aleta stared at her, surprised. "I suppose so— the stress and all. But what does that have to do with anything?"

Nancy shrugged. "Maybe nothing. But the police found some strands of red hair at Rudolph's place. They're going to do some tests on them. I thought you might like to know."

Aleta's face turned white. The intensity of her red hair and gold-green eyes was heightened by the sudden blanching of her complexion.

Nancy felt a twinge of sympathy for the young woman. Aleta wasn't very likable, but that didn't make her a murderer. "Look," Nancy said, her voice softening, "there's nothing necessarily incriminating about your visit to Karl Rudolph."

Aleta seemed to take strength from Nancy's

comment. "Of course not," she said firmly. "Joe and I went over there together—"

She stopped as the door suddenly creaked open. Aleta, peering over Nancy's shoulder at the intruder, turned even paler, her eyes wide with shock.

Chapter

Eleven

WHAT ARE YOU DOING HERE?" Aleta demanded.

Nancy turned just in time to see Joe slam the door behind him.

"What're you telling her?" he flung at Aleta. She took a step backward as if she'd been physically attacked.

Aleta's tone was defensive. "The truth."

"I thought we agreed on this when you called," Joe said in a low, hard voice.

So that's why Aleta was late meeting her, Nancy realized—Aleta had called Joe before coming over.

"I can explain," Aleta said.

Joe jerked his head in Nancy's direction. "She won't believe us."

"Try me," Nancy said.

Joe seemed doubtful. "Why should we trust you?"

Aleta spoke up. "Nancy told me the police found some strands of red hair at Rudolph's place. They're testing them."

Joe paled a bit, but he didn't back down. "Even if they match yours, that doesn't mean you were there last night."

"We have nothing to hide," Aleta snapped. "It's better to have it out in the open."

"I want to help—if I can," Nancy said.

Joe shrugged, as if washing his hands of the whole matter. He grabbed a small, straight back chair and straddled it, his arms crossed over its back. "Go ahead. Tell her. It won't prove anything either way."

Aleta explained that she and Joe had gone over to Rudolph's to try to convince him that Aleta had had nothing to do with leaking the story line. After all, she reasoned, she'd be stupid to do such a thing when she'd be the prime suspect.

"How did he react?" Nancy asked.

"He surprised us," Aleta continued. "He said he no longer believed that I was the culprit."

"He actually told you that?"

Aleta nodded. "He hinted that he had a pretty good idea who *was* leaking the information."

Joe picked up the story. "Karl wouldn't give us any more information on the source. But since he seemed friendlier, I asked if he'd be willing to modify his story line. He refused. He said he was sorry for Aleta, but actors knew this was one of the hazards of the business."

Nancy studied them, then turned to Aleta. "So Rudolph still planned to eliminate your role?" she asked.

Aleta nodded, and Joe added, "I told him about my idea, which would keep Aleta in the show and still provide a murder and a surprise ending. But just as I suspected, he wasn't interested. He was sure his story would win him another Emmy. And the publicity about the real source of the leaks would guarantee the show even higher ratings."

"But that doesn't mean we killed him!" Aleta exclaimed. "You don't kill a person over a story line!"

Joe stood up and smiled grimly. "People have killed for less than that. The point is," he continued, staring straight at Nancy, *"we* didn't kill him."

"You mentioned another Emmy," Nancy said. "Had Karl won before?"

Aleta looked shocked. "I can't believe you missed seeing it. Karl has a spotlight shining on it, right over the fireplace."

Nancy pictured the clean round spot, rimmed by dust, on the mantel. If that was where the Emmy had been, then where was it now? Had Karl put it away, or had someone taken it? The murderer?

"Do you think the police will believe us?" Aleta asked. "About why we were there? Rudolph was fine when we left."

Nancy said it would be in their favor if they went to the police. Before they did, though, she had one more thing to ask. She pulled the script from her large purse and handed it to Joe. "Do you know anything about this show?"

Joe glanced at the cover page. "This was done before I started working here."

Nancy persisted. "Do you know where I can get a video of it?"

Aleta glanced at the script, then said, "Yvonne might have a copy. Her husband wrote it."

"Writers sometimes save videos of shows they write. Sort of like a résumé," Joe added.

"Did Luther De Young get another job?" Nancy asked. She was beginning to wonder if Yvonne had an even stronger motive to get back at Rudolph.

Joe smiled, his lips twisting unpleasantly. "It's not that easy. There aren't that many writing jobs on soap operas. It's hard to break in and hard to switch shows. It's easier for actors."

"Oh, sure," Aleta said sarcastically. "Real easy."

Joe turned back to Nancy. "The fact is, on most shows the writers and the head writer make up a team. If the head writer leaves, he often takes his writers with him. So they move as a group. Then the new head writer comes in with his or her group. It's hard to break into that charmed circle."

"But you did," Nancy said.

Joe didn't smile. "Still seems like a miracle to me."

"A miracle that Rudolph fired Luther and that Joe was in the right place at the right time," Aleta said dryly.

Joe looked hurt. "You know I'd been writing scripts and story lines for a couple of years and sending them to Gardiner. I didn't appear out of nowhere."

Aleta touched his shoulder. "I'm sorry. I didn't mean to imply anything. I'm just so sick of all the tension." She picked up her jacket with the "Love and Loss" logo on the back. The shoulders were covered with strands of her hair, bright testimony to the tension she felt.

"Anyway, as I told you before, I've got an appointment," she said impatiently.

Nancy glanced at her watch. "I have to leave myself." It was time to meet Bess. She'd have to find Yvonne later. "Thanks for meeting me, Aleta. And thanks for your input, Joe."

They shook hands, and Nancy made her way back to the lobby of the studio. The same guard was on duty, still reading the same magazine. "I'd like to sign out," Nancy told him.

The guard slid the register over to her. Nancy glanced at the names there. Only Aleta and Joe were listed—both after her name. Whoever had been in the studio earlier had not signed in. "Did anyone else come into the studio earlier, besides me?" she asked the guard.

He turned the register around to read it. "Doesn't look like it."

"I mean, could anyone have come in and not signed in?"

The man straightened. "Not while I was on duty," he replied firmly.

"When did you come on duty?" she asked.

"At ten."

"Did you relieve someone else?"

"I didn't see him right away," he admitted, obviously hedging. "He could've gone to the men's room."

So someone could have sneaked in before ten, Nancy thought. "Thanks," she said to the guard, then pushed out through the door and searched the street for a cab. There wasn't enough time to take the subway, and Bess would start worrying if she didn't show up soon. A cab appeared going in the wrong direction, but the cabbie put on his brakes and did a U-turn in the middle of the empty street. Then he pulled up right in front of her. Nancy grinned and climbed in. "Nice driving," she said.

The driver rubbed his knuckles across his chest as if polishing a medal. "Where to?" he asked.

Nancy was just about to give him the address, when a movement caught her eye. She glanced back toward the building and saw Aleta hailing a cab. Nancy didn't hesitate. "Follow the cab that woman gets into," she said. "The one behind us."

"You're the boss," the cabbie replied, saluting.

Aleta's cab quickly pulled around Nancy's and took off. Nancy's cab kept right behind. They were heading south into Midtown traffic, and Nancy wondered how much longer they could tail Aleta's cab. Finally it stopped in front of an office building, but the woman who got out of the cab looked totally different from Aleta. For a moment Nancy thought they'd lost track of Aleta's cab.

The woman was a blond, her hair cut in bangs and a blunt cut that turned under at chin length. Also she wasn't wearing the logo jacket. Clutched in her hand was an overstuffed duffel bag, its zipper not entirely closed.

But there was something familiar about the way this woman walked, and the jeans and T-shirt were the same as Aleta's. Aleta must have donned a blond wig and removed her logo jacket. Obviously, the actress didn't want to be recognized.

That blond wig, Nancy decided, was hiding much more than Aleta's red hair.

Chapter

Twelve

NANCY ASKED THE CABBIE to wait and stayed in the cab while Aleta disappeared into the brick office building. All at once Nancy remembered why the building was so familiar. It was the home of Worldwide Broadcast. The last time she'd been involved in a case about a soap opera, the show had been *Danner's Dream,* and it was taped right there at Worldwide.

Nancy glanced at her watch. If she hurried, she might be able to beat Bess back to the apartment and change her clothes before Bess noticed their condition. Her mind was whirling on the trip downtown. How was Aleta connected to Worldwide?

As soon as Nancy entered the apartment, Bess

bounded out from the bedroom. "I did it!" she said, her blond curls bouncing with excitement. "I got us tickets for *Love Notes* tonight—" Bess broke off suddenly. "Nancy, what happened to you? Your clothes!"

Nancy tried to pass it off lightly. "Would you believe a dusty storage room, Bess?"

Bess eyed her suspiciously. "Should I?"

Nancy smiled weakly, pushing a strand of hair behind an ear. "No." She filled Bess in on the incident in the storage room.

"Let the police handle this," Bess said with a worried frown. "As of now, you're just a tourist in New York."

"That's not all," Nancy continued, knowing Bess's curiosity would win out. "I had a very interesting meeting with Aleta and Joe at the studio."

Bess's eyes narrowed. "They were in the studio —the same time you were?"

Nancy paused. "They didn't get there before I did." She told Bess the details of her talk with Aleta and Joe and then about Aleta's blond wig and destination.

"Do you think Aleta was auditioning for a role on another soap?" Bess wondered.

"Not on a Sunday," Nancy responded. "But then, who knows what's possible?"

"But why would she be so secretive? I mean, everyone knows she might lose her job."

Nancy was thoughtful as she headed for the bedroom. "There's another possibility," she offered.

Bess followed. "What's that?"

"*Danner's Dream* is in direct competition with *Love and Loss*. And *Danner's* is losing."

"You think—someone at *Danner's* is behind the leaks?"

"Like Gardiner told us. The name of the game is ratings."

"But why would Aleta agree to do it?"

"They could be dangling a job in front of her, or maybe in front of Joe," Nancy said, taking off her jacket. "He made a point of telling me how hard it is to get a job writing for daytime dramas."

"How're you going to find out if they're behind this?" Bess persisted.

"I'm going to have a nice little chat with Aleta, and I think she'll tell me everything we need to know."

"How can you be so sure?" Bess asked.

Nancy shrugged. "I'm not. And Yvonne—and Luther for that matter—aren't off the hook yet, either." Nancy headed for the bathroom. "Let's talk later, Bess," she said. "Right now I'd better shower and change. I'm really looking forward to relaxing and enjoying that show later."

"Me, too," Bess said happily. "The reviews

have been fabulous. They say it's the best love story since *Gone with the Wind*."

Later that night the girls were on the sidewalk in front of the theater after the show. "They were right," Bess said with a sigh. "Best love story I ever saw."

Nancy smiled. "I have to admit, I couldn't see how they were going to get the two leads back together."

"That's quite an admission for a detective, Nan," Bess teased. Then she added, "Actually, if they hadn't gone home to their tenth high school reunion, they never would have gotten together. They would have continued blaming each other for past mistakes." The two girls then climbed happily into a cab and returned home for a good night's sleep.

The next morning, Monday, Nancy insisted on returning to the studio. Gardiner was out of town for the day, but his secretary paged Sally, who came to Gardiner's office immediately.

Sally was shocked by Nancy's story of the attack and was inclined to agree with Bess that Nancy drop the case. The danger was too great. When Nancy said she just wanted to ask Yvonne about the missing tape, Sally grudgingly went along. Yvonne was directing that morning's episode, but Nancy might still be able to find her in her office.

"Just point us in the right direction," Nancy said. "We'll do the rest."

Yvonne was just about to leave her office when Nancy and Bess arrived. "I can't give you much time," she said in response to Nancy's request for a talk. "I'm shooting today."

Nancy pulled the script from her large carryall. "Your husband wrote this," she declared.

Yvonne reddened slightly. "So?"

"Mr. Gardiner asked me to investigate the leaks, and now, as you know, there's been a murder," Nancy said. "I understand that your husband may have had a good reason to hold a grudge against Karl Rudolph. I'd like to find out more about it."

"A grudge?" Yvonne said angrily, eyeing Nancy suspiciously. "That's ancient history. Luther's not connected to Karl's death, and there's no reason I have to talk to you about it."

"I thought you'd prefer talking to me than to the police," Nancy reasoned.

"Look," Yvonne said, sounding a bit more conciliatory. "I admit that Luther and I were very resentful when Karl fired him. It wasn't fair, but when was Karl Rudolph ever fair?" She paused for a moment, then added defiantly, "I know you're not supposed to speak ill of the dead, but Karl was always a dictator. Then, after he won his Emmy, he was totally unbearable."

"I take it you tried to get Gardiner to keep your husband on?" Nancy asked.

"Of course. I told Gardiner that Karl was just getting even because I recommended Aleta for the role. I told him that Karl hated not being in control of every last thing, including casting. But Gardiner wouldn't believe me."

"Why did Karl go after your husband and not you?" Nancy asked.

Yvonne pointed to a small glass shelf holding a familiar gold figure. "I won that Emmy for directing. Karl could only go so far and he knew it."

Bess looked up at the graceful statue of a woman holding a globe. "May I?" she asked.

Yvonne's face softened. "Sure. But be careful. It's heavier than it looks."

Bess hefted the statue and her eyes widened. "You're right. Very heavy—and very beautiful. And your name's engraved on it."

"The winner's name is always engraved on the Emmy," Yvonne explained. "And thank you—I think it's beautiful, too," she continued proudly.

Nancy smiled gratefully at Bess. Her friend had clearly put Yvonne in a much better mood. "Do you, by any chance, have the video of this show your husband wrote?" Nancy asked hopefully.

Yvonne hesitated, then said, "My husband probably has one stored at home. I'll call him to bring it over."

"Is there a tape machine handy?" Nancy asked.

"You'll need one of the tape machines in the booth," Yvonne replied. "They're the right size. But you can't use them until we wrap up today's shooting late this afternoon. I have to run now."

"We have a long wait," Bess said after Yvonne had left. "Do you think we can watch the show Yvonne's directing now?"

"Sure," Nancy said. "But first I want to stop by Rochelle's office. I'd like to see if she can remember who played the nurse on this show."

"The nurse?" Bess asked.

"All the regular performers in that episode are listed on the cover sheet by the names of their characters," Nancy explained. "But she's listed only as 'nurse,' which means she was probably a day-player."

"So?" Bess asked.

"So she's the only one who's unidentified. It may or may not be a lead. I can't know yet, but it's worth a try."

They found Rochelle in her office. She greeted them in her usual friendly manner. "What can I do for you ladies?" she asked.

Nancy once more fished out the script. "I'm curious about who played the nurse in this show."

Rochelle copied down the script number. "I'll check my files and let you know. It's a pretty old script, so I'll have to do some digging. Should I get the tape, too?"

"Yvonne's husband is bringing us the tape—

but we can't watch it until they wrap up today," Bess volunteered.

"But I'd still like to have the actress's name," Nancy added.

"No problem," responded Rochelle.

Nancy and Bess thanked her and headed off to the soundstage. They arrived just as Steve's scene ended. Just then Nancy felt a tap on her shoulder, which made her jump. Bess had to stifle a small scream when she saw her friend's sudden reaction. Then they both heard a male voice whisper, "It's just me, Zack."

The girls turned, and he beckoned them away from the soundstage. "Great seeing you again," he said directly to Nancy.

Nancy could feel her face heating up. "Great seeing you, too."

"Look, they'll be doing a couple more scenes, and then we're breaking for early lunch," Zack announced. "I hope you two will be my guests."

Bess chimed in, "We'd love to. Right, Nan?"

"As long as we don't have to skate there," Nancy said dryly. "I assume the limo is waiting."

"You're in for a treat," Zack said with a smile. "This time we're walking."

"My favorite mode of transportation," Nancy said. She had trouble speaking over the pounding of her heart and hoped Zack couldn't tell how excited she felt.

To Bess's delight, Steve joined them for lunch. Zack had chosen a small café nearby. "I recommend the *frittata*," he said, "if you like mushrooms, onions, and peppers. It's an Italian omelette."

"Sounds good," Bess said. "We didn't have time for a real breakfast."

Steve and Bess became lost in their own world. He'd ordered a waffle with ice cream and insisted that Bess have every other bite. "You're too thin," he told her fondly. Bess laughed with delight.

When they got back to the studio, Bess asked Nancy if she'd heard Steve's remark.

"Of course, I did," Nancy said with a grin.

"I thought you and Zack were too involved to notice anyone else speaking," Bess teased.

"Is that why you directed all your comments to Steve?"

Bess smiled. "He's very sweet. And who knows? Maybe I've been worrying about my weight all this time for no reason."

They returned to the set where Yvonne waved Nancy over. "My husband brought the tape for you," she said, adding graciously, "You can watch the rest of today's taping, if you'd like."

Nancy and Bess took Yvonne up on her offer. The taping ended early at four-thirty, and Nancy hurried to the booth to put in the tape. "Would you mind getting Sally, Bess?" she asked. "I want her to see the tape as soon as possible."

Nancy didn't want to frighten Bess, but she had a feeling that the tape held the answers to

Karl Rudolph's murder. Someone was willing to steal it from the storage room and harm her in the process, so obviously he or she was threatened. That meant time could be running out.

The booth was empty. Nancy looked around. Along one side was a large glass window facing out over the soundstage. From here, the producer and director could watch the taping. Above the window were a series of monitors, each screen connected to a camera onstage, showing what that camera was taping. In front of and below the window ran a large panel with switches that they used to choose which camera shots would be taped for final viewing. Along one wall were two more monitors connected to video recorders.

Nancy inserted the tape in one of the machines. She pressed Play and began watching a hospital scene. Before too long a blond nurse appeared in the background, but there were no close-ups of her. A few scenes later the nurse appeared again. This time the camera zoomed in on her. Nancy pressed the Pause button to get a better look. Something about the young actress was familiar, but the blond hair was wrong. Could it be a wig?

Nancy leaned forward to cover the actress's hair. When she focused just on the features, she gasped in recognition. A sudden noise behind her startled her. Expecting Sally and Bess, she said, "Look at this—" A painful blow to the back of her head stunned her, and she began to fall backward. Still conscious, Nancy struggled to get up, but she was shoved down. Something soft slid around her neck and was tightened. She clawed at her throat, trying desperately to breathe. Then she arched her back to grab at the hands behind her. She felt something swing hard across her head and then total blackness.

Chapter
Thirteen

NOISE AND THEN FINALLY VOICES came into focus through the gray haze in Nancy's head. "Thank God, she's coming out of it!" she heard Bess say. Then she saw Bess's worried face floating above her.

Nancy tried to touch her throat, but a hand caught hers. "It's all right, Nan. We're here." She recognized Sally's voice and then another face, Rochelle's, her forehead creased in a frown.

"Take it easy, Nancy. You've been hurt," Rochelle said.

Nancy felt an arm go around her waist. "Can you sit up?" Bess asked, trying to lift Nancy. Nancy tried to speak, but her voice cracked. She nodded, and Bess helped her to a chair.

"Do you know what happened?" Bess's eyes

were rimmed in red, tears still wet on her face. Nancy shook her head.

"You were so lucky, Nancy," Sally said. Nancy smiled wryly, and the dark-haired girl acknowledged the irony. "I know that sounds silly, but if Rochelle had showed up just a few minutes later—" Sally shook her head, paused, then went on to explain. Rochelle had come to the booth to give Nancy the information about the nurse on the show.

Rochelle chimed in, her voice low. "I was just putting my key card in the door of the booth—it shuts and locks automatically, you know. But the door was suddenly flung open, knocking me backward. So unfortunately, I didn't see who ran out. I was really angry and was about to follow him—or her—when I looked inside and saw you lying on the floor."

Bess picked up the story. By the time she and Sally arrived at the booth, the door had evidently swung closed again. Sally used her key card to get inside. The first thing they saw was Rochelle bending over Nancy, cradling her head. They rushed in, and Bess was just about to use CPR on Nancy when she moaned and started to awaken.

"Oh, Nan!" Bess cried, her voice quavering. "I really thought you were—" She stopped, unable to say the word.

"Well, I'm okay now," Nancy whispered, patting her friend's hand. She didn't want to dwell on her attack, and she was about to ask Bess to play the tape, when they all heard a key in the door and froze. Sally recovered first and quickly pushed the door open. Joe reeled backward.

"Hey! Watch it!" he yelled. Then he peered inside and saw the crowd gathered around Nancy. "What's going on?" he asked.

Bess eyed him suspiciously. Nancy read her thoughts. Could he have been her attacker? "Someone tried to strangle Nancy," Sally said.

Joe looked shocked. "Why?"

"I'm sure you don't know," Bess said coldly, ready to say more. Nancy squeezed her hand and Bess stopped abruptly.

"I'm sure I *don't* know," Joe responded testily. "Or I wouldn't have asked."

"We're just a little shaken up," Sally explained soothingly. Then she and Rochelle filled him in on the details, while Bess and Nancy watched his reaction. He seemed genuinely shocked.

"So, did you get to see the tape?" Joe asked when they were finished.

"Not all of it," Nancy whispered. "But enough." They all stared at her. "I know who played the part of the nurse."

"That's what I came to tell you," Rochelle interrupted. "I found her name in my files. It's a young actress, Ellen Powell."

Sally and Bess exchanged stunned glances. "Ellen?" they said, almost in unison. Then they looked to Nancy for confirmation. She nodded.

"Who?" Joe began.

"The girl you met at our table in the restaurant," Sally explained. "She's a friend of mine."

"She did tell us she'd had a small role—" Bess said, remembering.

"Before I came to work for the show," Sally finished.

Bess's expression mirrored Nancy's thoughts. Could Ellen possibly be involved with the leaks and with the recent attacks?

"I didn't recognize her at first," Nancy whispered. "She was wearing a blond wig—at least, I think it was a wig."

"It was," Rochelle said firmly. "As soon as I saw her name, I remembered. Karl wanted the nurse to be the focus of the scene, to distract the viewer from noticing what another character was doing. For some reason, he had envisioned the character as a blond. As you know, Ellen has brown hair. But she read so well that I told her if she'd wear a blond wig, I'd hire her." Rochelle smiled at the memory. "It changed her looks completely."

"It certainly did," Nancy whispered.

"Come to think of it," Rochelle said, "how did you ever recognize her? I wouldn't think her own mother would know her in that wig."

"I'll show you," Nancy said. Again she was about to ask them to play the tape, when they heard another key card in the door. They all waited expectantly. A head poked around the door. It was Yvonne. Her dark eyes widened. "What's going on in here?"

Bess and Nancy exchanged glances. The director and her husband had known that Nancy was going to be looking at the tape in the booth. Nancy realized that Yvonne's cooperation didn't necessarily rule out an attempt to get the tape back. "Something happened, Yvonne," Sally began.

"That's an understatement," Joe said.

"Will someone please fill me in?" Yvonne asked, exasperated.

Sally sighed. "Nancy was attacked."

Yvonne was visibly shocked. "Why?"

"That's what we're trying to find out," Nancy explained. She turned to Bess. "Check the machine," she whispered. "I hope the tape's still there."

Bess went over to look. "Someone took it," she said coldly, clearly considering everyone a suspect.

"I think we'd better call the police," Sally said.

"I agree," Rochelle said. "They could check for fingerprints."

"That'll help a lot," Joe added sarcastically. "Everyone's fingerprints will be in the booth."

Nancy caught Bess's attention and pointed to her throat. "Did you find whatever was tied around my neck?" she asked in a whisper.

Bess acted stricken. "Oh, gee, Nan. We didn't

even look." She glanced around. "There are so many cables and wires around here. Any of them could've been—" She stopped when Nancy shook her head vigorously.

"It was some kind of cloth," Nancy whispered. "Like a scarf. Or a stocking."

"I'm really sorry," Bess said. "The person who ran out probably took it, along with the tape."

"The police are on their way," Sally said.

"Did you see a scarf, or anything that could've been tied around Nancy's neck?" Bess asked her.

Sally reacted just as Bess had. "I never thought to look. But Rochelle might've seen something."

Rochelle couldn't help. "I think that Nancy's attacker heard me fumbling at the door. I had some trouble inserting my key card because I was carrying my big duffel. That gave the person plenty of time to untie whatever it was and take it along." She touched Nancy's hair lightly. "I'm sorry I didn't get here sooner."

Suddenly Detective Asher loomed in the doorway, where Joe had propped open the door. He came right over to Nancy. "Are you okay?"

Nancy nodded.

"Someone tried to strangle her," Bess said.

"That's what I was told," Asher said. "You never bought the burglar theory, did you?" he went on, eyeing Nancy. She shook her head. "Well, we don't, either—anymore," he told her. At Nancy's questioning look, he added, "There was an old coin collection in his closet. Any burglar worthy of the name would have found it." He paused. "And, of course, we found the murder weapon."

"The Emmy," Nancy whispered.

The detective looked disappointed, his surprise spoiled. "How'd you know?"

"That circle in the dust on the mantel," Nancy said. "I found out Rudolph's Emmy had been kept there. And I learned that his name was engraved on it. So I figured a burglar wouldn't steal it."

"Right. Hard to pawn," Asher said.

"Where'd you find it?" Nancy asked.

"Would you believe in the trash? A few blocks away. We found Rudolph's blood on the base."

"But how will that help us find the killer?" Bess asked. "And why would that person try to kill Nancy over a stupid tape? We can always find another copy."

Asher answered for her. "Whoever is behind this believes Nancy is too close to solving the case, tape or no tape."

"Do you know who did it, Nan?" Bess asked, shocked.

Nancy shook her head.

"Doesn't matter," Asher interjected, glancing slowly around the room. "Our killer has decided that Nancy will definitely figure it out."

Especially, Nancy thought, since she now had one more piece of information. She had a vague memory of having touched something smooth and hard, with a rough edge, like glass and metal. It could have been a watch on the attacker's wrist. She almost smiled at the irony of it—a physical reminder that time could be running out—for both herself and the mastermind of the leaks.

Chapter

Fourteen

Back at their apartment, Nancy rested on a plaid sofa, eating frozen yogurt that Bess had bought to soothe her throat. Bess sat next to her, writing postcards. After finishing the last spoonful, Nancy checked the phone number Sally had given her, then punched in the digits. Ellen answered on the first ring.

"Ellen," Nancy said into the phone, "this is Nancy. Can you do me a favor?"

When Nancy explained that she needed a copy of Ellen's appearance on *Love and Loss,* Ellen said, "Gee, Nancy, I'd love to help, but I left all my copies of that show with various casting directors. I'll try to get one back, though."

After Nancy had hung up and reported Ellen's

part of the conversation, Bess was quiet and thoughtful. "It's possible she's sincere," she said. Then she held up a postcard showing a New York City horse and carriage. "I thought George would like this card. We still haven't taken a carriage ride around Central Park."

Nancy smiled and took the card from Bess. It reminded her of the photograph on Rochelle's desk. Her young daughter was also standing next to a horse and carriage. But there was something different about this one. Before she could decide what that might be, Bess plopped another postcard in front of her. "Isn't this one great? It's a copy of the poster of the Broadway show we saw, *Love Notes.* I'm sending it to my mom and dad."

Nancy now held one postcard in each hand. The horse and carriage—and the theater poster. The teasing in the back of her mind grew stronger. What was the connection? She shook her head and started on a new tack. Conover. She'd wanted to question him from the beginning, but had put it off for one reason or another. What was his role in all this? she wondered. She resolved to find out right then.

She reached for the phone directory and looked up *Soap Talk*'s address. It was on Broadway, near the Premiere Broadcast building.

"Bess, I've got to talk to Conover—the reporter for the soap magazine," she said. "I know he probably won't reveal his source for the leaks, but he still might drop a clue. At any rate, talking to him can't hurt—we might at least get him to explain why he followed us on Friday."

"I don't know, Nan," Bess said anxiously. "You say it can't hurt, but I think you ought to put this investigation on hold. I—"

"Bess," Nancy said, interrupting, "the only way to protect myself is to figure things out fast—before another attempt is made."

Nancy phoned *Soap Talk* to see if, on the off chance, Conover was working late since it was after office hours. Nancy was surprised when he answered his own phone and agreed to see them.

A short fifteen minutes later, Conover came out to the reception area and led them back to his office.

"So how can I help you, ladies?" he asked.

"We'd like to know why you were following us the other day," Nancy said.

"Us?" he asked, confused. "I happened to follow you," he continued to Nancy, "because of the redheaded woman with you. I thought I knew her, but I was mistaken."

Nancy had a flash of understanding. "You thought she was Aleta McCloud," Nancy said flatly, indicating Bess. "You thought she might have had some new information for you about the *Love and Loss* story line. But it was really my friend Bess here in a red wig."

"I'm not saying Aleta is my source," Conover said testily, "but what if she is? She's not breaking any laws, and neither am I."

There was a quick knock at the door, and a woman in a large red hat entered. Conover stood up. "These ladies were just leaving, Monica," he said.

The woman, wearing a chic black suit with red collar and cuffs, barely glanced at them before saying, "I thought we were going to dinner." She went out, shutting the door behind her.

"That was my editor," Conover said coldly, "which means I have to go have dinner with her."

In the cab back home Bess said excitedly, "So Conover basically admitted that Aleta is the source for the leaks."

"Yes," Nancy said thoughtfully. "He did. But I still have trouble believing that Aleta would act so rashly—after all, she'd be the obvious suspect."

Nancy mulled over the case for the remainder of the ride home. They picked up Chinese food to take home and plopped down on the twin sofas to eat. Finally feeling a bit restored Nancy sat forward and focused on Bess. "Do you remember when Steve put that red wig on you?" she asked.

Bess smiled, remembering. "Yes, but what does that have to do with anything?" she asked.

"Sally told us that soap opera shows like to find look-alikes if possible when they're recasting."

Bess grinned. "You aren't suggesting that I have a chance to get Aleta's part, are you? Besides, that role is about to become history, given the story line."

"But not if Rudolph was forced to change his story line. Then a look-alike could step into Aleta's part."

Bess chewed her lip. "But there'd be no need for a look-alike. Aleta would just continue to play it. Unless it can be proved that she's the source of the leaks—then she'd be fired."

"That's just it. If she were discredited and fired, her part would open up for someone else."

"But Rudolph himself admitted to Aleta that he knew she *wasn't* leaking the information. But then Conover hinted that she was!" Bess's brow furrowed as she tried to puzzle out the case.

"Well," Nancy said, propping up a pillow behind her, "we have only Aleta's word that Rudolph had decided she was innocent. But even so, I believe her."

"So why would Conover have wanted to talk to Aleta the day he followed us, if she wasn't the source of the leaks?" Bess asked.

"Suppose," Nancy offered, "that someone was impersonating Aleta."

"Oh," Bess said. "You mean, someone wearing a red wig could've leaked information to Conover? And he might have thought he was talking to Aleta if it was dark enough?"

"Right."

"But how would Rudolph know that?" Bess wondered. "Conover never revealed his source."

"He knew a columnist wouldn't print something unless he believed he was talking to a real member of the show," Nancy explained. "My theory is that Rudolph saw someone who looked like Aleta talking to Conover. And so at first Rudolph would have assumed it *was* Aleta."

"Then what would have made him change his mind?" Bess asked.

"Rudolph also knew that Aleta would be the logical suspect. Her role was being eliminated. So for her to leak the information would be risky and stupid. It's also possible that the disguise didn't fool Rudolph, but he wasn't sure who she really *was*."

"So you're saying," Bess went on slowly, "that this person was setting Aleta up in order to get her fired *before* Rudolph could kill the character? In order to take her place?"

"It's just a theory," Nancy said.

"The actress wouldn't have the part for very long," Bess pointed out. "The role was ending."

"She would have the part if the leaks forced Rudolph to change his story line and let the character live," Nancy explained.

"Oooh," Bess said. "And then the look-alike would have the role at least until Karl had figured out another way to kill Laura."

Nancy nodded. "And the look-alike could figure that Rudolph might like her and decide not to kill off the character."

"But that still doesn't explain Rudolph's death," Bess pointed out.

"Maybe the look-alike was getting frustrated

that Rudolph was refusing to change the story line. Or maybe when Rudolph found out who the culprit really was, he confronted her and threatened to expose her and destroy her plans."

"And what about your attack, and the stolen tape?" Bess asked. "How does that figure in?"

"I'm not sure, Bess," Nancy admitted, hoping that Ellen had nothing to do with the case. "I'll have to think some more about why the tape is important."

Bess shook her head. "I don't know," she continued. "There's still your theory that Aleta was working for the other soap—and leaking the story line to help them in the ratings. That way, if Karl's new story line is changed, she keeps her job. And if it's not changed, she gets a job on the other show."

"Well, Bess, as you say, these are just theories. That's why I've got to talk to Aleta. I've got to find out what she was doing over at *Danner's Dream.*"

"You don't quit, do you, Nan?" Bess said fondly. "I just hope you don't get hurt again."

"I'll be careful, I promise," Nancy assured her. "But right now, let's get some sleep. I'm totally exhausted."

The next morning Nancy awoke first. She dressed quietly and wrote Bess a note explaining what she wanted her to do. She felt good, knowing she could depend on her friend this way. After shutting the bedroom door, she made three phone calls. The first was to William Pappas, the producer at *Danner's Dream*. "I owe you a favor," he admitted. "What can I do for you?"

"If you happen to have a tape that Ellen Powell left with you, could you send it over to me at *Love and Loss*?" Nancy asked. Pappas promised to check, and also acknowledged that Aleta McCloud had auditioned for his show.

Nancy then called Detective Asher. "I think Mr. Conover may be helpful to us," she said, filling him in on her talk with Conover. She also described to him what she saw on the tape the day before. The two of them then discussed looking for more evidence in Rudolph's offices— both at work and at his brownstone. "Then," Nancy continued, "would you ask Mr. Gardiner to have everybody present in his office in a couple of hours, or whenever you think you'll be ready?" Nancy asked. "I'll take care of the rest."

"Will do," Asher replied. Nancy and Asher talked for another minute, firming up plans before hanging up.

Nancy's last call was to Aleta, whom she arranged to see shortly. Then, after eating a quick bowl of cereal, she took off for the studio.

Aleta was waiting in her dressing room. She appeared concerned as she expressed her sympathy and outrage over what Nancy had suffered. Nancy reminded herself that she was talking to an actress. Aleta also expressed surprise that Nancy was still involved after her attack.

"I just want to tie up a few loose ends," Nancy said. "I'm not putting myself in danger."

"I hope I'm not one of your loose ends," Aleta said, smiling. "As you suggested, Joe and I told Detective Asher that we'd seen Rudolph the night he was killed. I even gave him some strands of my hair to test. It's getting embarrassing how much hair I'm losing from this ordeal."

Nancy quietly dropped her surprise bombshell. "Did you also tell him you were auditioning for *Danner's Dream*?"

The shocked expression on the other woman's face was answer enough. "How did you know about that?"

"I followed your cab Sunday."

Aleta's complexion almost matched her hair. "How dare you!"

"As I said, loose ends," Nancy responded coolly.

"Well, if you think you've uncovered some kind of plot, you couldn't be more wrong." Aleta's voice was shrill with outrage. "Yes, I was auditioning there. They set up a special audition on Sunday for me because I'm busy here all the time. I have to protect myself and get work. Karl was killing me off in a matter of weeks."

"I'm not accusing you of anything," Nancy said. "Though you certainly seemed at pains to hide your identity."

Aleta rolled her eyes. "They preferred a blond for this role."

"How'd the audition go?" Nancy asked casually.

Aleta's eyes narrowed to green slits. "Why do you care?" she asked.

"Did they promise you a job—if your character does get killed off? Or if you get blamed for leaking that ending?"

Aleta looked disgusted. "I began auditioning before the leaks started."

That was the information Nancy was really after, and she hit Aleta with it. "That means," Nancy stated carefully, "you knew ahead of time that your role was ending."

Aleta seemed ready to deny it, but then she shrugged. "Yes. I knew. But I didn't talk with any reporter to save my job. I began doing what any actor does, auditioning for more work."

"A reporter named Conover from *Soap Talk* seems to think he's met you. What reason would you have to meet with him, other than to provide the leaks?" Nancy countered.

"Conover claims he's met me? That's absolute rubbish!" Aleta said hotly. "I've never set eyes on him. And, frankly, I never want to! He must be mixing me up with someone else."

"Did *Danner's Dream* ask you to leak the story line, to hurt the ratings at *Love and Loss?*" Nancy asked, trying another tack.

"Of course not," Aleta snapped. "I can't believe this," she continued impatiently. "I'm the victim here. My role is being cut. But I'm being blamed for everything that's gone wrong."

"Was it Joe who gave you that advance information?" Nancy asked. "About your character being killed?"

Aleta looked defeated. "He was trying to protect me. Neither of us ever dreamed there'd be story leaks. We were sure my role was ending."

"But," Nancy pointed out, "if the leaks forced the story line to be changed, then Joe's story would be used instead. It sounds like he had a lot to gain."

"He wouldn't have leaked Karl's story," Aleta said plaintively, "especially since he knew I'd be suspected. And besides, I told you that Karl had figured out the guilty person, and he no longer thought it was me—or Joe for that matter."

"We have no proof that he really told you that," Nancy pointed out. Without waiting for a response, she rose and headed up to Gardiner's office. She saw Joe at the other end of the hallway on the third floor. He was approaching her slowly, his face a mask.

"You really like to live dangerously, don't you, Nancy Drew," he said, his eyes glinting. "Or maybe you don't like living at all."

Chapter

Fifteen

I'M NOT IN DANGER ANYMORE," Nancy responded calmly, hoping she'd guessed right about Joe. "Mr. Gardiner's expecting me."

"I know." Joe didn't move out of the way. "He called and asked me to be there. I figured you had something to do with it."

"Is that what you meant by my living dangerously?"

"If someone had tried to kill me in the studio yesterday, you can be dead sure I wouldn't be here in the morning," Joe said wryly. "Unless you have all the answers now."

"I don't," Nancy said with a smile. "But I will."

The door at the end of the hall opened and

Sally's head appeared. "Nancy, Joe, we're in the conference room. Come on in."

Joe followed Nancy into the room. Besides Gardiner, Sally had assembled Yvonne and Rochelle as Nancy had directed. "Did you put the tape in?" Nancy asked.

Sally nodded. "We're ready to go."

Nancy turned to the others. "I just want you to see a few scenes. It won't take long."

When they came to the scene with the close-up of Ellen, Nancy pressed the Pause button. "That's Ellen Powell," she said. "Tell me if you see a resemblance to anyone else."

They all huddled around the television screen. "With all that blond hair . . ." Gardiner began, shaking his head doubtfully.

Nancy cupped her hands around the girl's face, blotting out the hair. All at once Yvonne reacted. "She's the spitting image of Aleta!"

Joe whistled. "Amazing!"

"What's so surprising about that?" Rochelle asked. "I keep a file of look-alikes, just in case we need them. There are lots out there."

A knock on the door interrupted them, and Gardiner's secretary came into the room. "Detective Asher is here," she announced. They all turned, surprised. Gardiner said, "Show him in."

They seemed even more surprised when Ellen entered with the detective. Ellen immediately turned to Sally. "What's going on here, Sally?

This man said it was your idea to have me brought here." Then she noticed the television screen and paled a bit. "You found a tape, I see."

"Yes," Nancy said. "Your tape, actually. William Pappas sent it over."

"He shouldn't have done that," Ellen protested. "It's my property."

The others were now staring at Ellen. With her brown hair in a ponytail and little makeup, it was almost impossible to see her resemblance to Aleta. But Joe was nodding his head slowly. "I thought you looked familiar," he said. "That time in the restaurant."

"Ellen told us she had nothing to do with leaking any story material to that magazine columnist," Asher said.

"Of course I didn't," Ellen said angrily. "I didn't have any information to leak!"

Asher raised an eyebrow, and Gardiner opened the inner door leading from the conference room to his office. "You can come in now, Mr. Conover."

A murmur went around the room. They all recognized the name of the columnist. When Conover entered, he passed a knowing look with Asher. Then his expression hardened. "I demand to know why I've been summoned here!" he said loudly. "I've committed no crime."

"Maybe not," Asher said. "But it's possible that the leaks your column has been printing may be connected to a homicide."

Nancy noted the shock on Ellen's face. Or was it fear? She couldn't be sure. The others didn't appear particularly surprised. After Rudolph's death and the attack on Nancy, they were almost immune to shock.

Asher went on. "Would you mind telling us who is the source of those leaks?" Conover appeared to be uncomfortable, but Asher persisted. "I don't think this is the time to get squeamish about revealing names, Mr. Conover."

Conover glanced briefly at Gardiner. "I've met a few times with Aleta McCloud."

This time, Nancy noted, most of the faces expressed shock. They hadn't expected their suspicions to be so readily confirmed. Ellen seemed more relieved than surprised, Nancy thought. Asher thanked the man and asked him to wait in the next room a little longer. Conover nodded, not meeting anyone's eyes, and left.

Gardiner then walked to the hall door and opened it. All eyes were riveted on the doorway, prepared for anything. Nancy tried not to smile as Bess entered, wearing her cap with the red ponytail. She winked at Nancy. Bess was also wearing her new cardigan sweater and was carrying a shopping bag. A murmur again swept the room when they saw a sullen Aleta following close behind Bess.

Nancy took the shopping bag from Bess and

removed a red wing. She held it out. "Would you mind putting this on, Ellen?"

When Ellen hesitated, Detective Asher repeated the request. His tone made it plain that he expected her to comply. Ellen reluctantly accepted the wig and plopped it on her head, not bothering to arrange it correctly. Asher then opened the other door and called Conover back. "Would you mind pointing out the girl you've been meeting?" the detective asked.

Conover shrugged, then glanced around the room. His gaze fell first on Bess, who was standing in his line of sight. "She looks familiar."

"Anyone else?" Asher asked.

As Conover hesitated, Ellen pulled off the wig. "This is ridiculous," she said. "I've done nothing wrong, and I refuse to join in these stupid games."

Conover turned and pointed to Ellen. *"She's* the one I've been talking to. I recognize her voice."

"Didn't you notice that her voice was different from Aleta's when you met?" Nancy asked.

Conover's eyes shifted nervously. "Okay. I finally knew she wasn't Aleta, but her stuff seemed to be accurate. So I used it. I don't care who it comes from."

"Is that why you stared at Aleta in the restaurant?" Nancy persisted. "Because when you saw her, you realized you'd been meeting with someone who was pretending to be her?"

Conover nodded. "You seem to have figured it all out. Yeah. I'd just talked to this girl here"—he indicated Ellen. "Then when I saw Aleta in the restaurant, she was wearing something totally different. That's when I was sure what was going on." He turned to Aleta. "Actually, I thought I might be doing you a favor, Ms. McCloud. If the writers had had to change the ending, you could've kept your job."

"Don't do me any more favors, Mr. Conover," Aleta said coldly. Then she turned to Ellen. "And you—why were you trying to ruin me?"

"I wasn't," Ellen said defiantly.

"Are you denying you met with Daryl Conover?" Asher asked her.

All at once Ellen began crying. "Yes, I met with him. But that's no crime. And it had nothing to do with Karl Rudolph's death."

"But why?" Sally asked. "Why would you do such a thing? I thought we were friends."

"It had nothing to do with you," Ellen said.

"The main question," Nancy said, "is how Ellen got the information about the story line."

"How about it, Ellen?" Asher asked. "Who told you what was going to happen on the show?"

They all waited—the room utterly silent.

"I just figured it out," Ellen said after a long pause.

"Oh, come on," Joe said. "You weren't guessing. You knew."

"It seemed logical to me that Laura would be killed off," Ellen insisted.

Nancy decided it was time for the rest of her plan. She nodded to Bess, who pulled out the framed photograph of the little girl from Rochelle's desk. She handed it to Nancy who brought it over to Rochelle. "This picture of your daughter—it's ten years old, isn't it," Nancy said flatly.

"Why would you take my photo without asking me?" Rochelle demanded.

Nancy ignored that remark and went on. "Look at that bus, right behind the horse and carriage. There's a poster on it advertising a new Broadway show, *Dance Dance Dance.*"

Rochelle stared at the photo. "So?"

"That show opened ten years ago and has closed since," Nancy stated. "My father took me to see it when we visited my aunt. Which would make your daughter about nineteen now."

"I never said that was a recent picture of my child," Rochelle said, not missing a beat. "But in this industry, being young is considered a virtue. So I let people think my daughter was still only nine years old. What's the harm?"

Nancy then brought the picture over to Ellen, whose face was still slippery with tears. Nancy held the photo up to her.

Chapter

Sixteen

THIS IS A PICTURE OF YOU, isn't it?" Nancy asked.

There was a moment of shocked silence, then murmurs of surprise greeted Nancy's statement. Ellen glanced at Rochelle. The older woman answered for her. "Yes, Ellen's my daughter."

Once more Sally turned to her friend, angry and hurt. "Ellen," she began, but she couldn't continue. Nancy could see how betrayed Sally felt.

Ellen reddened. "I'm sorry," she said. "When I came here from California, Mother said I'd have a better chance if no one knew we were related. Especially if a part opened up on this show."

"Or you could *make* a part open up," Nancy countered. "When your mother learned about the new story line, she decided it was your big chance to step into an existing role. *If*—and that was the big *if*—two things were accomplished. First, force Karl to abandon his story line by leaking it to the magazine, so that the character of Laura would be continued. Second, frame Aleta for the leaks so she'd be fired."

Nancy turned to Rochelle and continued. "And then you, as casting director, could put Ellen in Aleta's role. Her resemblance, of course, made your job easier."

Aleta was furious. "Rochelle knew Rudolph would grab at any excuse to get rid of me." Then she cast a disdainful look at Conover. "I bet Rochelle even took pictures of Ellen talking to this creep, so she could say it was me."

Rochelle's reaction showed that Aleta had hit a bull's-eye. "I'm very sorry this happened," she said stiffly. "But I committed no crime."

"Not until Rudolph figured out what was going on," Nancy said.

"What makes you think he did?" Rochelle's tone was arrogant now. She was taking the offensive, Nancy realized.

Detective Asher spoke up. "We found a pile of photos in Rudolph's office. They were spread all over his desk."

"It's a miracle you could find anything in his office," Joe said.

Asher smiled. "We might not have, if Nancy hadn't told us what to look for."

All eyes turned to her, as Nancy explained. "It's not unusual for a head writer to keep a file of résumés to glance through when he's thinking of adding a new character. When we were in Karl's office, I noticed the head shots on his desk."

Asher continued. "So Nancy called me this morning and suggested that we take a look in Rudolph's office for a head shot of Ellen. We found Ellen's picture, with her résumé attached to the back. It included her appearance on *Love and Loss*. As Nancy suspected, something must have clicked for Rudolph, something that made him go home to watch the show."

Nancy nodded to Bess, who once again reached into the shopping bag and pulled out the yearbook and typed play that Nancy had seen on Rudolph's desk.

"Thanks to Detective Asher," Nancy went on, "some important evidence has come to light— from Karl Rudolph's high school yearbook and a play he wrote at that time."

"It's called *The Evil Twin*," Bess threw in. "About one twin impersonating her sister in order to pin a crime on her."

"A familiar story line," Nancy added.

Gardiner shook his head. "You've lost me."

"I sympathize." Nancy chuckled. "I couldn't put it together until I remembered how strange it seemed that Rudolph would have his high school yearbook out the night he was murdered. I asked Detective Asher to check it out for me, and he discovered that Rudolph's play had been put on in his senior year."

"And a budding actress named Rochelle Powell had played the twins," Asher finished.

"Powell?" everyone chorused.

"So what?" Rochelle blurted out. "I've already admitted I'm Ellen's mother. Ellen simply decided to take my maiden name as her stage name."

"Rudolph saw Ellen's name on the back of her head shot and made the connection," Nancy continued, ignoring Rochelle. "The play, the twin story line, the name *Powell*. Then, when he watched the tape to confirm his suspicions, he saw Ellen's resemblance to Aleta. That cinched it for him. Then, of course, he called Rochelle," Nancy concluded.

"I told you about that call. We were talking about some other day-players." Rochelle managed to sound indignant and hurt, as if she were being unfairly accused.

Asher went on as if Rochelle hadn't interrupted. "Once Rudolph told you that he knew what you and Ellen were doing," he said to Rochelle, "you told your daughter to visit him. A pretty girl can often be persuasive."

"I never went to his home," Ellen protested hotly. "And I can prove it." She pointed to Sally and Nancy. "We all had dinner together."

"But you left early," Sally pointed out.

Ellen persisted. "I told you. I had to go home to prepare for an audition."

"But you can't prove that, can you?" Asher said, trapping Ellen. "I think we have enough to book you on suspicion. You had motive—and opportunity."

"I didn't have a motive to *kill* the man," Ellen whimpered. "My only motive was to get the part."

"Your motive was to shut Rudolph up," Asher said. "Once he'd figured out your plan, he was a real danger to your career. Once he'd let the word out, no one would ever hire you, or your mother, again."

Asher took out a pair of handcuffs and headed in Ellen's direction. The frightened girl cast a pleading glance at her mother. Rochelle blocked Asher's way. "My daughter was not the one who went over to Rudolph's home."

"Who was?" Nancy asked quickly.

Rochelle was just as quick with her reply. "Joe and Aleta."

Nancy followed up instantly. Everything depended on her playing Rochelle just right. "How do you know that?"

"I overheard them talking about it."

"That doesn't cut it," Asher said. "You have no proof. You're obviously trying to protect your daughter." Asher had reached Ellen by now and was putting her hands behind her back.

"But I saw them!" Rochelle blurted. "I saw them leaving his home!"

This was the moment Nancy needed. "You saw them when you were hiding under the stairwell." Rochelle seemed stunned as Nancy went on. "You waited until they left, and then Rudolph let you in and you killed him."

"No, no." Rochelle's hands fluttered before her face, the topaz ring catching the light. "It was an accident. A terrible accident."

Once more a shocked silence filled the room. Nancy glanced at Ellen and saw the blood drain from the girl's face. Nancy stepped up her attack. "Was hurling that grocery cart at me an accident?"

"She said she was just going to scare you," Ellen blurted out. "I swear. Or I never would've—" She broke off.

Nancy completed it. "Or you never would have arranged for her to follow us."

Now Rochelle hurried to explain. "It was just a warning. I meant no one any harm. Not even Rudolph. You were right about him watching that tape," she continued. "He phoned me in a fury, threatening to ruin Ellen's career. He wouldn't listen. So I went over there to reason with him, to plead with him. After all, Ellen is only nineteen. It was all my idea. She shouldn't have to suffer."

A moan interrupted Rochelle's outburst.

Ellen's green eyes, so identical to Aleta's, were riveted on her mother.

"I'm sorry, darling," Rochelle said. "But you'll understand when I explain. I tried to reason with Karl. But he was raving like a madman. He said Gardiner had warned him that he still might have to drop his story line, a story line that would have won him another Emmy. Then he grabbed the Emmy from the mantel and shook it in my face, accusing me of wrecking his career. I pushed him away, and he dropped it. Then he came at me with his fists. I was afraid. I picked up the Emmy. He was still raving. I was only trying to stop him. I didn't mean to hit him that hard. But it was self-defense. I couldn't reason with him at all."

Nancy felt no sympathy. "Like you tried to reason with me by trying to crush me in the storage room? And by trying to strangle me in the engineering booth? Are those examples of your reasoning powers?"

Suddenly Bess spoke up, her gaze fastened on Rochelle. "It was you," she said in a hoarse whisper, her voice trembling. *"You* tried to kill Nancy!" Nancy put an arm around her friend, calming her.

"She would have succeeded, Bess," Nancy said grimly. "If you and Sally hadn't come along just in time. So she had to pretend she was saving me instead. Somehow, in the midst of all that—

probably when she heard your voices outside the door—she managed to grab the tape and stuff it in her bag."

"But why was it so important to Rochelle that you not see the tape, Nancy?" Sally asked. "After all, you didn't have Karl's inside information about the play with the evil twin."

"At that point, Rochelle wasn't sure what information I had. She was desperate for her plan to succeed," Nancy explained.

"And how did you come to realize your attacker was Rochelle?" Sally asked.

"When I was reaching behind me," Nancy explained, "trying to grab whoever was holding me, I felt what I thought was a piece of glass and metal. Maybe a watch."

Bess's eyes widened. "Her ring. The topaz we admired."

Nancy nodded, continuing. "I was also trying to dig my nails into her hand. I didn't know for sure if I'd scratched it or not." Rochelle had plunged her hands into her pockets as Nancy was speaking. But when they all looked at her, she held them out defiantly. A thick red welt ran across the back of one hand.

"I did this at home," she said. "My daughter can verify that."

"Mother!" Ellen screamed, her face contorted. "You said you were only going to warn her—" She broke off, overcome.

Nancy followed up. "Warn me the way you did, Ellen, by nailing that note to our door?"

Ellen nodded, shame and sorrow written on her face. "Mother suspected that Mr. Gardiner had called you in."

Rochelle's shoulders slumped momentarily. Then she straightened and stared coolly at Nancy. "I knew my daughter could be a great actress. All she needed was a chance. I could give her that. I could give her the opportunity I never had."

Nancy couldn't help feeling sorry for Ellen. The girl rubbed her eyes, as if hoping to wake from a nightmare. When Ellen spoke again, her voice was not much above a whisper. "My mother told me we weren't breaking any laws. Aleta was going to lose her job, anyway. So we weren't really hurting anybody."

"Just ruining Aleta's career," Joe said, biting off the words. "That shouldn't hurt much."

Ellen covered her face with her hands, but Rochelle came to her daughter's defense one last time. "Aleta would never have had a career if Yvonne hadn't interfered. She was the one who brought that girl to Mr. Gardiner's attention. I never would cast her against Rudolph's wishes."

"Because you were waiting to cast your own daughter instead," Nancy said. She turned to Bess. "I think it's time for us to be tourists."

Bess squeezed her hand. "I'm ready."

"Good," Asher said. "I'll take it from here."

Asher and another detective who'd been waiting in Gardiner's office led Rochelle and Ellen out of the room.

When they were gone, Aleta touched Nancy's arm. "I really owe you," she said, and this time Nancy was sure Aleta wasn't acting.

"Me, too," Joe said. "In this business, you sometimes lose your ability to trust. I'm sorry I gave you such a hard time." He and Nancy shook hands.

Mr. Gardiner thanked Nancy profusely, apologizing for the dangers she had been exposed to while helping him out. "I hope you don't think this sort of thing goes on here all the time," he said.

Nancy smiled. "Nope. Just on soap operas."

As they left, Bess said, "Sally wants us to meet her after work at that cappuccino place."

"Back where it all started," Nancy said with a grin.

Back at the apartment Nancy treated herself to a long nap. When she woke, she found Bess holding up a red silk minidress, apparently deciding what to wear. Nancy smiled to herself, guessing what was in store. When Bess suggested that Nancy wear her pink cotton sweater, Nancy knew for sure. She also felt she knew what Bess was carrying in a small, wrapped box.

Just as she suspected, Steve and Zack were at the cappuccino place with Sally. Steve waved cheerily as Nancy and Bess came in. Zack was concerned. Was Nancy really recovered from her ordeal? he wanted to know. And why hadn't she told him what was going on?

"I didn't know myself, most of the time," Nancy responded, amused. "But I'm fine. Honest."

"Hey, what's in the box, Bess?" Steve asked.

Bess handed it to him and spoke softly. "Something to remember me by."

Steve opened the box and, as Nancy had guessed, pulled out the ponytail cap. He popped it on his head immediately. "This is the real me," he said. Then he reached for Bess's hand. "I'll think of you every time I see a redhead." They all laughed.

Then Zack turned his dark eyes on Nancy. "I don't need anything to remember you by," he said in a low voice. "You're impossible to forget." Then he added, "As I bet someone at home already knows."

Nancy hesitated. Zack wouldn't be easy to forget, either. But she was going home in a few days, and Ned would indeed be waiting for her. At the thought of her boyfriend, she felt a familiar surge of affection. "Yes," she said gently. "His name is Ned."

Zack held up his cup of espresso. "To Ned," he said. "A very, very lucky guy."

Nancy's next case:

Nancy's in Belize, on the Caribbean coast of Central America, to visit Ned on holiday—a perfect opportunity for romance. But perhaps not with each other! While tensions rise between Nancy and Ned, a different and more pressing kind of threat approaches from offshore—a gang of pirates hijacking million-dollar yachts! Nancy's never heard of a more bizarre band of buccaneers. Setting the yacht owners adrift in fully stocked lifeboats, they also pierce the right ears of the men aboard each yacht and insert a gold earring. The pirates may not be as polite as they seem, though, as Nancy soon discovers. For not only is her relationship with Ned at risk—so is her life . . . in *Captive Heart,* Case #108 in The Nancy Drew Files™.

THE HARDY BOYS CASEFILES